THE BLOOD OF THE BRAVE

Betty Baker

THE
BLOOD
OF
THE
BRAVE

HARPER & ROW, PUBLISHERS
New York

To Mom

Contents

Author's Note

MEXICO, IN THIS BOOK, refers only to the city-state in the lake and Mexicans means only the Aztecs who built the city and ruled most of the country now called the United States of Mexico. Except Mateo and One-Eye, every character may be found in the records of the conquest. Some, like Aunt Maria, are only names appearing unexpectedly. The words and deeds of Father Olmedo and Ortega's son, who became a page to Montezuma, are faithfully recorded by Bernal Díaz. Every account of the Cortez expedition mentions the greyhound found alive and well on the island, but there is no record of her name, owner, or fate. From these bits and pieces of history the characters grew and this story was woven.

*"Gold is, in its last analysis, the sweat
of the poor and the blood of the brave."*

JOSEPH NAPOLEON

Chapter One

THE DISCOVERY

THE LARGE BIRD perched on a limb high above the entangling vines, preening its bright green feathers and grumbling to itself. Juan glanced at his two companions. Mateo had already wound his crossbow and was fitting a feathered bolt to the string. Diego watched, posturing like a bored don at court, one hand on his hip and the other resting on the hilt of his small sword. Neither seemed to feel the pity that touched Juan's heart.

He looked again at the unsuspecting parrot, torn between his desire for food and his sorrow at seeing such a beautiful creature die to provide it. He could jostle Mateo's arm at the moment of firing, but then he'd go empty all day with only cassava bread for supper. The idle soldiers in Santiago had hunted this part of the island for sport as well as food. There was little chance they'd find other game so near the town.

As Juan wavered between heart and stomach, the dog at his side whimpered.

"Easy, Boba." He touched the tense neck to silence her.

In that second Mateo fired. The bird plunged into the tangle of vines. The greyhound charged forward.

"After her," yelled Mateo.

"There's no need to exert ourselves," said Diego. "The dog will fetch the bird."

Mateo laughed. "Not this dog."

Juan tore aside the tropical growth, guided by the growls. Mateo helped him pull the greyhound from the dead parrot.

"And you consider that a hunting dog?" sneered Diego.

Juan held the mangled bird above his head. The big dog pranced and wagged her tail proudly.

"Good girl," murmured Juan, patting her head.

"Good?" shouted Mateo. "She's chewed the feathers off my bolt along with half the bird. That dim-witted animal will never make a hunter. You should have let the Indians eat her."

Juan rubbed the dog's ears. Though she was not full-grown, he had to raise his hand to pat her head. Her tongue lolled out in a smile and the long skinny tail whipped his legs as she doubled around him in her joy. Leave Boba for the Indians to eat? Never!

"She's still young," he protested. "I've only had her six or seven months. How long since Díaz sailed with Hernandez?"

"Only a few days lacking seven months." Diego was a

page at the governor's palace. Such items rolled easily and accurately from his tongue.

"I traded with the Indians for Boba just before Díaz left. She ate the tassels on his dress sword, I remember. So she's not more than nine months old."

"Old enough to be trained if you intend to use her for hunting," insisted the page.

Mateo had taken the parrot and was stripping the feathers expertly. "Maybe you can teach her to run down Indians or stand guard duty. Though by St. James' beard, she'd eat the entire camp out of food before dawn."

"She just chews because she's growing." And like many in Cuba, she never had quite enough to eat. Juan didn't mind for himself, but he pitied the dog.

"You'd better face up to it," Mateo continued. "You made a poor trade. The buttons she cost you at least held your doublet decently closed. This dog is good for nothing."

"She is!"

The other two laughed. "For what?"

Juan sighed. How could he explain what Boba meant to him? The dog was the first real friend he'd ever known. In Castile his domineering Aunt Maria had kept him walled off from the world. Here in Cuba there were few boys his age. Most children were young, of recent marriages. Those who sailed to Cuba were of fighting age, or like Diego.

He glanced at the page, resplendent in smooth hose

3

fastened by red garters to his slashed breeches. The blue velvet doublet matched the broad soft hat. Juan's legs and feet were bare and his shabby doublet pockmarked by sparks from his father's forge. Though the same age, the boys were not friends. Diego's position was no barrier, for his father was not a don. Nor did the page's fine clothing matter. Juan had worn some as good or better and preferred his present shabbiness. The trouble lay in Diego himself. Or perhaps it was just that Juan's father had ordered him to be courteous to the governor's relative.

Mateo interrupted Juan's thoughts. "Give me your sword, Diego."

The boy's hand went to his waist. "Why should you want my sword?"

"Come, boy. We need a spit to roast this bird."

Diego's mouth opened and closed soundlessly. At last he stammered, "My sword for a spit? How dare you! Not only is such a request insulting, the steel would weaken in the fire."

"What if it does? It's only a dress sword. And I haven't heard that your uncle permitted pages to wear them."

"I will not always be a page. I'll soon be of an age to follow the king's pendant. A soldier's sword goes to no one, least of all a crossbowman."

"A soldier!" Mateo rocked back and forth with laughter. "Juan, did you hear? This young popinjay thinks he's a soldier."

4

"He's right in a way. Don't we all owe allegiance to King Charles?" Juan took the page by the elbow. "Come, we'll gather wood for the fire."

He pushed through the undergrowth, searching out dead vines and fallen branches not yet dank and rotting. Diego tried to keep pace but his sword caught at every turn and he walked in great circles to avoid tearing doublet or hose. He was less than no help. His rambling doubled the swarms of gnats and mosquitoes Juan would have stirred up by himself. But the search for fuel kept the page and crossbow-man apart while the bird was spitted on a green stick and roasted.

Boba did not leave the cookfire. Each time Juan left an armful of sticks beside Mateo, the dog whimpered and thumped her tail as if begging him not to order her to follow. Juan had thought the heat would drive her away but the small fire was lost under the Cuban sun.

At last Mateo called them to eat. Juan settled beside his dog, confident Diego and the young soldier couldn't quarrel with their mouths full. He was mistaken.

They had hardly torn the bones apart when Mateo winked at Juan and said, "It must have been hard soldiering in the old days."

"The same as today, I guess," Juan said quickly. He glared a warning at the older boy but Mateo ignored it.

"Yes, sir, I guess the Lord grew nobles different then.

Gave them long legs like deer and lots of wind, though they still have the wind and to spare, heaven knows. Only now they use it to talk your ears to nubbins."

Diego looked bewildered. Juan made a big fuss over moving the food out of Boba's reach, hoping the distraction would keep the crossbowman from continuing. Juan couldn't yet see where the talk was headed, but he was sure it would end in another fight.

"Yes, sir, a different breed of men in the old days," Mateo repeated.

"How so?" asked Diego.

"They had to be. How else were they to hunt unless they could run faster than the game? You must get within biting distance to use a sword. Of course the crossbow has changed all that. With a few good crossbowmen along, the army eats well."

To Juan's surprise, Diego agreed. Then he added, "But hunting is all a crossbow is good for."

"The crossbow is the mainstay of the army. Without it Cuba would never have been conquered. There's nothing like a barrage of arrows to discourage the Indians."

"The crossbow is a coward's weapon."

"Coward!" Mateo shook the leg bone at the page. The greyhound snatched it deftly from his fingers, but Mateo gave the dog only a glance. "How can you call me a coward?"

"It is easy. I have only to look at you."

6

Juan stepped between them. "You know that's not true, Diego. And Mateo knows very well that the nobles' swords and lances are as important in battle as the crossbow."

Shouts of denial drowned his words. Juan searched frantically for something to distract them.

"If ever there was a coward's weapon," he yelled, "it's the arquebus."

There was silence.

Mateo slapped him on the back. "Well said, Juanito. Those hand guns are as useless as Boba. The battle is over before they are ready to be fired a second time. Gunpowder weapons will never be of any use to the soldiers of Castile."

"It's all the same," said Diego. "While the arquebusiers are fiddling with rods and powder the crossbowmen are scrambling about the ground searching for some small necessary part they've lost from their machines. In the meantime the swordsmen and lancers are protecting both of them."

"Why, you overstuffed squeak mouse, what do you know of battle? The only time you'll ever draw blood is if you trip over that useless sword."

Juan was struggling to keep the dog from gobbling everything in sight. "Have done," he shouted at the squabblers.

Diego turned his back. Without a word of farewell he pushed through the rough-leafed palmettos. Clutching the squirming dog, Juan watched the page stride angrily down the trail toward Santiago. He turned on Mateo.

"When you find a gap in the armor, you never stop prodding, do you?"

"Ah, he turns my stomach with his airs."

"True, but Governor Velásquez is related to his mother."

"So?" The crossbowman picked up the carcass and turned it over in search of a morsel the dog had overlooked.

"So my father's been waiting for the governor to sign his land grant. It was promised to him when he helped Velásquez conquer Cuba."

"That was six years ago. By now the governor's relatives have grabbed all the land and slaves. Your father will work that forge forever unless he listens to reason and takes up his crossbow again."

Juan shook his head. "Father has refused to join any expeditions. Even Díaz couldn't persuade him."

Though worry lay heavy on his shoulders, Juan helped Mateo pick the bones clean. Santiago swarmed with soldiers who wanted dents removed from cuirasses and helmets or a new lance hammered on the forge. There was plenty of work for his father but the soldiers paid only with promises. The next expedition, they said, was sure to discover new lands of great wealth. But the lands discovered so far were poorer than Hispaniola and Cuba. Worst of all, most of the soldiers perished from starvation or poisoned arrows. Only when a plantation owner brought a load of gold ore to be smelted did Juan and his father eat well. And now there was Boba's huge appetite to satisfy.

8

He jumped to his feet. "Where's Boba?"

Mateo yelled. "She's chewing my crossbow! Is there nothing this dog won't eat?"

"Nothing of which I know." Juan leaned over anxiously. "Is it badly damaged?"

"Just a few teeth marks. I can always tell how a huge beast attacked me and I slew it with my bare hands. And I'll show the tooth marks as proof."

Juan grinned. It was just the sort of thing Mateo would do. As he followed the crossbowman along the path, one eye on the dog nosing for lizards under rotting bark and leaves, Juan wondered why the bowman had offered his friendship. Was it because Mateo was younger than most foot soldiers in Santiago? Though older than Juan, Mateo shared more interests with the boy than with the idling adventure seekers that gathered in Santiago. Both liked to roam the island, hunting and exploring while the soldiers loafed in the wine shops or swapped stories at Juan's father's forge. There were even times like today when Juan felt older than his friend. Why did Mateo always bait the page?

Juan had known it was a mistake to invite Diego to hunt with them, but the page had delivered a commission from the palace and lingered in the doorway of the forge listening to their plans. There hadn't been anything for it but to ask him along. Juan had even thought it might help his father's cause if he was friendly with someone near the governor. Instead he'd made it more hopeless.

The path turned dusty beneath Juan's bare feet as the trees thinned and the patches of sunshine grew larger. He quickened his steps, eager for the cool shade of Santiago's narrow streets. Mateo also hurried as they neared the Rat Nest, a scattering of mud and thatch huts hastily built by soldiers needing shelter until they signed for an expedition. As Juan's father often pointed out, many signed and left; few returned. But a continual stream of adventurers from Castile kept the Rat Nest overcrowded.

Boba raced off to search the huts.

Mateo grinned. "She'll find nothing here. We've already roasted or boiled everything we can spare, save for an old leather wrist-guard we're keeping for a feast day."

"Where is everyone?" asked Juan. Never had he seen the Rat Nest without groups of men arguing, gaming, or dozing against a shaded wall.

"Where they always go. The wine shops or your father's forge. Still, it is strange that we've seen no one."

The bowman strode past his own doorless hut. Juan called Boba and they followed Mateo through the crumbling mud wall that had protected Santiago in the early days of conquest. Rows of small shuttered buildings kept the dog at Juan's heels until they entered the plaza. Juan stared in amazement. It seemed that everyone in Santiago had crowded into the marketplace. People huddled together, talking excitedly and waving their arms. A horseman on the other side of the square shouted for them to make way but was ignored.

"Something has happened," said Mateo.

"They all seem to be watching the governor's palace."

Mateo grabbed his arm. "Come, let's go ask Diego what it's about."

"I don't think he'll speak to us now."

"Why not?"

Juan shook his head. The young soldier never held a grudge and so never expected anyone else to nurse their injured feelings. Before Juan could explain, the page raced out of the rambling one-story palace.

"Ho, Diego," called Mateo. "What passes?"

The page sauntered up, his chin held high like a governor inspecting swine. "So when you need information you must come to your superiors."

Juan kicked Mateo to silence him and said quickly, "Not at all, Diego. We saw all this excitement and wondered about it. Who, we said, would be in such an honored and trustworthy position that he could enlighten us? Who, we asked ourselves, could give us the true facts and not a pack of rumors? Immediately we knew only our noble friend Diego was cut to measure."

"Take care," muttered Mateo. "Liars burn in hell."

Juan kicked him again.

Diego glanced suspiciously from one to the other, but his own excitement broke through the arrogant pose. "The Hernandez ships just sailed in from Florida."

Mateo made a noise of disgust. "I thought something of importance had been done. There is nothing in that forsaken land of swamp and palmetto worth hoisting sail for."

The page's doublet swelled importantly. "Oh, they didn't explore Florida. They just came home that way because it was shorter."

Juan stared at Mateo but the bowman looked as bewildered as Juan felt. The expedition had sailed south, hoping to find lands beyond Darien.* There was no place they could have returned from that would be shorter by way of Florida. No *known* place. But if a storm had blown them off course, blown them far north and perhaps westward as well, they would certainly have sailed east and sighted Florida.

"They've done it!" cried Juan. "Don't you understand, you great lump of slow-wittedness? They've found the great North Sea, or El Dorado, or the lost Atlantis."

"Glory be to God," murmured Mateo, crossing himself reverently.

Juan did the same, silently offering a prayer of thanks. A thousand questions burned his lips. Had they found gold? Or the fierce six-headed monsters many claimed lived beyond the sea? Did the men there have wings? Were they giants or only six hands high with two eyes on one side of the head and none on the other? Anything was possible in this great new world God had revealed to His favored men of Castile.

"Captain Hernandez was badly injured," Diego con-

---

* Panama

tinued. "He landed at Sancti-Spíritus where he has a planta-tion, but the rest sailed on to Santiago."

"Never mind the captain," said Mateo. "Tell us about this new land."

"Oh, then you don't wish to hear about the chest?"

"What chest?" chorused the two listeners.

"The one just brought to the governor."

Mateo grabbed Diego's blue doublet and shook it. "Out with it! Stop tormenting us with bits and scraps."

Juan pushed between them. "Leave be, Mateo."

It took many honeyed words to undo the damage. By the time Juan had soothed the page, the horseman had forced passage through the square and was dismounting at a crowded wine shop. Diego pointed to the rider.

"There is Cortez. I have an urgent message for him from the governor." And he ran off, leaving Juan and Mateo in ignorance.

They wandered back and forth through the plaza, squeez-ing into one group after another, catching bits and pieces of conversation. The mysterious chest was said to hold pearls as large as marbles. Others said gold ingots or jewels of unbe-lievable value. There was talk of magnificent carved statues and a city of stone pyramids that the explorers had chris-tened Great Cairo. The lost tribes of Israel were mentioned more than once.

"I wonder how much of this is true and how much wishful dreaming," muttered Mateo.

13

"There is one way to find out. Díaz was with the expedition. He'll come to see father as soon as he's free."

"Then let us go to your house and wait."

Juan looked about for Boba, but the dog had wandered off on some quest of her own. Santiago was such a small village even a dog of her little intelligence could find her way home. He led the way down a narrow street, through a bare courtyard, and into the kitchen. They stood ankle deep in the litter of daily living and listened for movement in the mud-brick house.

"Father?" called Juan.

Laughter drifted across the court.

"They're in the forge. Come."

The sun-baked courtyard felt hot as a forge until Juan stepped into the forge itself. He blinked in the sudden darkness, surprised that the usual company of idling soldiers had disappeared. But they would not think to wait for Díaz. At the first rumor of gold they would rush to the plaza.

Juan's father, his face tinged red by the glowing coals, nodded at the wall behind Juan. "Have you no greeting for an old friend?"

Juan turned. A young swordsman, clothes stained and beard untrimmed, lounged just inside the open door.

"Díaz!" Juan flung his arms around the soldier. "You've returned."

"Did you doubt that I would?"

Juan pulled away from the welcoming embrace. "Did you

really find pearls as large as my fist? Did you find the lost tribes of Israel as they say?"

"Is there to be another expedition to Great Cairo?" put in Mateo.

Díaz laughed. "One at a time. Sit and I shall tell you of wonders beyond your unlikeliest dreams."

"Will you make empty-headed fools of them too?" demanded Juan's father. He slammed a piece of iron on the forge and beat it with his hammer.

"Stop that noise, Ortega. How can I tell of the great discovery with you pounding away? Come and listen."

"Don't think you will tempt me with your fancy tales." But he put aside his tools and sat on a cask near the boys.

Juan leaned forward eagerly. The soldier rubbed his hands.

"Now," he said, "we begin."

Chapter Two

THE PRAYER

Juan's mouth dropped slowly open as Díaz moved through the story of the voyage. A great storm had blown them off course and it had been twenty-one days before they sighted land.

"There before us rose a great stone pyramid such as those at Cairo. None of us had seen such a large city in Hispaniola or Cuba. The natives came out in boats hollowed from a single log and each large enough to carry forty warriors."

"Ha!" scoffed Mateo. "You expect us to believe that?"

"I knew Bernal Díaz in Castile before either of us came to this new world," said Juan's father. "I have never known him to speak anything but the truth. If he says the log boats were that large, then that is the way they were."

"Go on," urged Juan.

"They invited us ashore, and since they seemed peaceful we launched our small boats and canoes. But they led us into an ambush." He shook his head. "Never have I seen Indians fight so well. But when our crossbowmen let their arrows fly, the Indians pulled back."

Mateo jabbed Juan so hard he nearly toppled from his perch on the wobbly cask. "What did I tell you? There are other people I could mention who should be hearing this."

"Hush, Mateo. Let him finish."

Díaz frowned at the young bowman. "We swordsmen took the brunt of the attack. We fought hand to hand. Our captain suffered ten wounds. He is dying from them."

"And you, Díaz?" asked Ortega.

The soldier waved his hand. "A few scratches only."

"They must be mighty scratches to make you move so stiffly. Don't think I haven't noticed." Juan's father shook his head.

"Only an arrow between the ribs, but all that is nothing. Let me tell you of the temple in the center of the town. *Cúes* they call these pyramids. In it we found heathen idols finely carved but stained with blood. There were also ornaments and offerings of gold."

He held up his hand at their cries. "Not fine pure gold but worked by skilled craftsmen. Father Gonzales took the ornaments back to the ships. Also we captured two Indians and baptized them. All were delivered today to Governor Velásquez."

Then he told how they'd sailed up the coast, finding other cities larger than Great Cairo and natives who wore fine robes and feathers.

"But the Indians were hostile and our water was nearly

gone. Our pilot assured us Florida was near and we sailed there to fill our casks. A mistake, for we lost good men to the savages there."

He was silent a moment, then added, "I am sure if we could have sailed but a little farther up the coast we would have reached the North Sea and opened the way to China."

"But there is gold to be had?" asked Mateo.

Díaz nodded. "Governor Velásquez is organizing another expedition. He has asked me to go as ensign."

"Fools," snorted Ortega as he worked the bellows. "The lot of you are fools. You fight all your lives and have nothing but scars to show for it at the end. It is better to get a piece of land and make something of yourself."

"You have less chance of getting land in Cuba, old friend, than I have of loading myself with gold in Great Cairo."

"I'm going," cried Mateo. "I'm going with you. What about you, Juan?"

"No," shouted Ortega. "I'll not have my son killed by starvation or poisoned arrows as all those men were in Darien."

"But this is different from Darien," protested Juan. "You heard Díaz yourself."

"We'll stay here."

"But the governor will never sign your land grant."

"My crossbow helped him take Cuba. He owes it to me. He'll sign as soon as there are enough Indians found to work another plantation."

Which would be never, the way the Indians were dying. As soon as they were taken from their villages they began wasting away. Juan tried to keep his disappointment from showing. Mateo patted his shoulder. Just then a gray form hurtled through the door and leaped on Díaz.

"Down, girl," Juan ordered.

With one last lick at the soldier's face the dog obeyed. Díaz clapped a hand over his nose.

"Whew! What has she been rolling in?"

Boba's neck was coated with manure. She sat grinning at them, pleased with herself, for horses in Cuba were scarcer than nuggets of gold.

"She does that to protect herself in a fight," explained Juan.

Mateo hooted. "That beast fight?"

"How you can bear to have her sleep with you is beyond me," grumbled Ortega.

"Have you found a name for her?" asked Díaz. When Juan told him, he laughed. "And who named her a dunce? You, Ortega?"

Juan's father bent over a pile of iron scraps, his back toward them. "It is a fitting name," he muttered.

Boba wagged her tail and took a nip at the edge of the soldier's breeches. Díaz pulled her ears thoughtfully.

"Juan," he said at last, "a good greyhound is useful on an expedition for hunting and guard duty. Since you can't join us yourself, why not lease me Boba on shares?"

19

"That dumb dog?" Mateo howled with laughter.

"She isn't dumb," said Juan.

"Then why did you name her Boba?"

"I like the sound." And his father had called her a dunce so often she would answer to nothing else. "She'd be a great help on the expedition, only I couldn't bear to part with her."

Mateo planned to go with the next expedition. If Boba went too, Juan would be lonely again. Even more lonely now that he'd had the dog's constant companionship. He just couldn't part with her. If only his father would dust off his crossbow. He'd fought valiantly once, for God and King Charles.

Seven years ago they'd come to Hispaniola, only to find the land already parceled out to the noblemen. Ortega had joined Velásquez in the conquest of Cuba, which was the last time he had followed the resounding battle cry of Santiago, for St. James.

Juan grimaced at the memory of those days. In Castile he'd lived with his dead mother's sister. He'd succeeded in forgetting everything about Aunt Maria except the booming voice that had been forever ordering him about. In Hispaniola he'd again been left with aunts. They were softer, kinder women, but it had still been a world of "Keep your hose smooth," "Don't soil your doublet," and "Mind your manners." Though his father hadn't received the promised plantation, life here was more to Juan's liking.

He ate when he was hungry or when the opportunity

arose. He dressed as he pleased, and when he threw himself on the rumpled bed there was no nonsense about hanging up his clothes or even removing them. When the dirt in the house made walking difficult they simply threw the trash into the courtyard. A good simple life. Though he could have done with more food and a warm cloak, Juan wouldn't trade his life for anything except a chance to take part in a new conquest. There'd be no aunts or cousins to leave him with. His father would have to take him. But could he persuade his father to go?

In the months that followed, Juan argued and pleaded. He even resorted to tears, a weapon he hadn't ever used with Aunt Maria because he'd known it wouldn't have worked with her. It didn't with his father either. That day he simply ordered Juan to take himself off to the small hut behind the church.

"The new friar has asked for an interpreter to accompany him on his rounds of the Indian villages," said Ortega. "You have a quick ear for Indian tongues."

"May I take Boba?" The dog would enjoy the trips as much as he would.

"Yes, and be sure you translate accurately. It is the only way we have of paying Father Olmedo."

"Paying him for what?"

"For the lessons he's going to give you. Your mother came from a good family. She would want you to have an education."

But Father Olmedo greeted Juan with, "We will begin

with Latin. Listen well, my son. It is the only means I have of repaying you for interpreting my sermons."

Juan considered trying to untangle the confusion of who was paying whom for what. Then he remembered his aunts and decided not to bother. His father was as determined to educate him as his aunts had been to keep him clean and mannerly. At least he could walk fast and shorten the lessons. That was one advantage boys in Castile didn't have. Except for the never-ending Latin, history, and catechism (which Father Olmedo stopped when he discovered Juan could recite it in Castilian and two Indian dialects) Juan and Boba looked forward to the trips around the island.

Only when the expedition's four ships sank low in the harbor with the weight of provisions did Juan begrudge the time spent away from town. So little time was left to persuade his father to change his mind.

"Must I go?" he'd ask when the friar summoned him.

"Yes!" shouted his father. "By Job's boils, you're driving me mad with your constant badgering about the expedition. Be gone!"

In spite of Juan's pleading his father remained firm. The expedition would sail without Ortega. Nothing but a miracle would change his mind.

Juan lay in bed, Boba's heavy weight pressed against his side. Yes, a miracle was what he needed. He crossed himself and began a prayer to St. James, then changed his mind and directed his plea to St. Jude. St. Jude interceded only in the most desperate and hopeless situations. Juan thought his qualified, though he had doubts as to whether it was important enough to warrant a miracle. But if he and Díaz together hadn't been able to stir his father, what could, except a miracle?

"And as a favor, St. Jude, hurry," he added.

There were only four days left before the ships sailed.

Chapter Three

ST. JUDE'S ANSWER

J UAN HAD KNELT in the rear of the church so as to be first outside after mass. He'd debated repeating his request to St. Jude and decided against it. If his plight merited the saint's attention, one prayer was enough.

Boba bounded up from the patch of early morning sunshine where she always waited. Side by side they ran across the plaza to the food stalls.

General Grijalva had picked half the island bare buying provisions for the expedition. Not many of the stalls set haphazardly between the rows of wine shops had food to sell, but those few weighted the cool spring air with the odor of roast pork and fresh loaves of cassava bread. Juan drew long, slow breaths. It was the nearest he would come to eating that morning unless one of the open stalls belonged to One-Eye. Though Ortega gave credit freely to the soldiers, he would ask credit of no one but One-Eye, his old comrade in arms.

Juan sighed as he dragged Boba from a rack of dried fish and hurried her toward the old soldier's bread stall. If

Ortega could collect but half of what Grijalva's soldiers owed him, Juan and his father would have ripe melons for breakfast, chicken for supper, and warm cloaks for the rainy season. It was some comfort to know that most of Santiago was also depending on Grijalva's success.

Only one of the four men already at One-Eye's stall had money for bread. The half-blind merchant argued and complained even to the one who paid. Juan shuffled his bare feet impatiently as he waited his turn. He was to meet Mateo soon at the harbor.

One-Eye made a face at Juan's request for credit. "I haven't two maravedis to clink together in my purse. Everybody wants credit, even General Grijalva."

Boba nibbled at one of the flat loaves. One-Eye rapped her nose smartly with a twig and the dog scuttled off. Juan stared longingly after her. He hated this daily haggling, but they must have bread.

"My father has been mending cuirasses and making lances for the soldiers but—"

"Ha! There's no profit in that," interrupted One-Eye. "Oh, they tell you they're coming back with the ships awash from the cargo of gold. To hear them, El Dorado is just over the horizon. But has there been one expedition that hasn't ended in disaster?"

"The last one led by Hernandez."

One-Eye spat contemptuously. "Ended in debt. The gold hardly paid for the bacon. They didn't bring a single slave either. Too pious to slave hunt, they were."

25

"This time they'll be successful."

"Only if God is willing."

Juan shook his head. "Father says they're all fools chasing ghost fire in the swamps. Díaz and I have both begged him to join but he says he will wait here for the land Governor Velásquez promised him."

"Ha! We'll wait as long for that as for the soldiers' gold. Six years since we helped Velásquez take Cuba, and I'm here at my stall and your father's still at his forge. Fools? Ha! We're two of the biggest."

Juan glanced at the sun, anxious to be off. "Will you give us credit? Any day now a plantation owner is sure to bring a load of gold ore to be smelted. We will pay you then."

"Gold ore that your father and I should own. But no, the governor must provide for his swarms of relatives first." He shook a bony finger at Juan. "Mind me, boy. If ever you join an expedition be sure the commander is an orphan."

The sun was high enough to warm him by the time One-Eye finished grumbling and gave him the cassava bread. He looked around for Boba and saw her circling Father Olmedo and Bernal Díaz. As Juan neared them the dog stretched out on the ground and began gnawing at the hem of the friar's robe.

Father Olmedo pushed the dog gently away and smiled at Juan. "If this beast doesn't lose her taste for clerical vestments, you'll have to leave her at home. My frock is as ragged as a palmetto."

26

"Now you see the trouble you will save yourself if you let me take her along," said Díaz.

Again Juan refused.

"You're as hard to persuade as Father Olmedo."

"I have work to do here," said the priest. "The Indians have suffered needlessly. They no longer have the will to live. So long as I have Juan to speak for me I shall continue my efforts to ease their plight."

The priest blessed Juan and Díaz, patted Boba and hurried off to his hut behind the church.

"A good man," said Díaz. "But wasting his efforts. Nothing can be done now for these Indians." Then he smiled down at Juan. "If you should change your mind, my offer of shares still stands."

"Many thanks but I won't change it. Come, Boba."

"Go with God."

Juan repeated the parting phrase and hurried across the square and down the dusty street.

The kitchen was empty. Juan kicked aside the rubbish on the floor, set the bread and the clay bottle of thin sour wine on the table, and called his father to breakfast. Ortega stared gloomily at the meager food.

"And I left Castile to make a better life for us."

"It is a better life." Juan bit his lower lip. He should have agreed with his father and urged him again to join Díaz and Mateo.

"Your mother came from a fine family. Her sister treated

you like a nobleman's son. With her husband's wealth and influence she might have found a nobleman to take you as a page." He sighed. "Your Aunt Maria could have done much for you."

"I thought you left Castile to get away from her."

"It's true she is forceful in her ways and sharp of tongue, but a fine and generous woman all the same."

"Then let's go back to her."

"Never!" roared his father, then grinned sheepishly at Juan's laughter. "Where are you off to this morning?"

"I'm to meet Mateo at the harbor."

But at that moment the young bowman ran through the court.

"Run," he shouted. "She is coming here, but if you hurry there is still time to escape."

"Escape what?" asked Ortega. "Who is coming?"

Mateo babbled on as if he hadn't heard. "You have never heard such language and such a voice to shout it with. Any captain would be proud to have it. It is said she put down a mutiny with her lung power alone, though the sailors vowed if she had sailed with them past Santiago, they'd have thrown her overboard."

"Who?" Juan demanded. None of the few women in Santiago would visit the forge.

Mateo rushed back to the gate in the courtyard wall. "Too late. You are trapped."

Juan and his father crowded up to the opening. A tall

spare woman dressed in black swept into the street from the square. Three sailors loaded with baggage staggered ahead of her swinging walking stick.

"Drop one of those and I'll have you quartered," boomed a voice that could not possibly come from such a thin woman but did. "Dunderheads! Dolts! Watch where you're going."

She swished the cane again. One sailor scraped a wall, hopping out of the way, bringing a fresh outburst at his clumsiness.

"May the saints have mercy on us," breathed Ortega. "It's your Aunt Maria."

"Well, we can always sail in three days."

"No!"

"Then just tell her to go back where she came from."

His father spun him around. "That is enough of that, Juan. You will obey your aunt and make her welcome. Our house is hers."

"But you left Castile to get away from her."

"Boy, if you wish to keep your tongue you'll forget you ever heard those words."

Ortega greeted the strident woman and led her into the house. Mateo sniggered when she thundered, "Do you always entertain guests in your pigsty? Surely no human lives here."

Juan's father mumbled an answer.

"I knew it," Aunt Maria shouted in triumph. "When my

poor husband died, my thoughts turned immediately to my dear sister's family. 'Maria,' I said to myself, 'you must go to them. They need the guiding hand of a woman. That child needs a woman's tenderness.' "

There were thuds as the sailors unloaded.

"Watch what you're doing with that box, you unshod excuse for a mule."

The sailors fled through the courtyard. Juan grabbed Boba's loose neck skin in one hand and Mateo's arm in the other.

"Run," he ordered.

"But I want to hear more. What a captain she'd make."

"And she'll be looking for foot soldiers to sweep and scrub."

"In that case, retreat is the order of the hour."

They headed for the harbor to watch the soldiers enlist under Grijalva's banner and count the boatloads of supplies rowed out to the ships. Low clouds darkened the midday sky. Juan shivered in the chill seaborne gusts but it was easier to bear the weather than Aunt Maria's tongue. Mateo coaxed a ride to the ships in return for loading provisions. Juan would have liked to join the bowman but he couldn't leave Boba alone on the wharf. He settled behind the water barrels to wait. Boba huddled against him for warmth. When the rain began, Juan could think of only two places to find shelter: home and Father Olmedo's hut.

The priest's home was not much better than an Indian's.

But there was a fire and the roof did not leak too badly near it. When Juan offered to decline irregular Latin verbs, Father Olmedo raised his eyebrows but asked no questions. After vespers, Juan met Díaz in the plaza and the soldier invited him to supper at the wine shop. Though he lingered over the meal, Juan was at last forced to go home. He walked slowly, watching Boba, fat with roast pork, splashing happily in the puddles. Their entrance into the newly scrubbed kitchen was greeted with a shriek.

"You can't bring that dirty beast in here," said Aunt Maria.

"How else is she to reach the bedroom?" asked Juan.

"There is no need for her to reach the bedroom."

"But she sleeps with me."

"Not that filthy creature."

Juan looked to his father for help but Ortega refused to meet his eyes.

Juan tried again. "It gets cold at night. Boba keeps me warm."

His aunt sniffed. "You're cold because you haven't proper curtains around your bed. I shall take care of that tomorrow."

"Then Boba can sleep with me tonight?"

"Definitely not. Out with her."

Aunt Maria reached for her cane. Juan grabbed Boba and took her into the courtyard. But the greyhound barked steadily for what seemed hours to Juan in his clean cold bed.

He heard the shuffle of feet from his aunt's room, then the creak of the outside door.

The barking stopped. Juan sat up.

Had she killed Boba? He wouldn't put it past her. Then a heavy body heaved onto the bed and a cold nose nuzzled his hand over the sleek head.

Aunt Maria's raspy voice filled the room. "She goes out first thing in the morning and stays out."

Snuggling contentedly, Juan whispered, "Boba, you're misnamed. No dog who can get her own way with Aunt Maria is a dunce. You're the smartest dog in the world."

Boba licked his face in agreement.

Juan was up before dawn, hoping to sneak away, but Aunt Maria was already at the fireplace. She rattled off a list of chores that would keep him busy all day. The only compensation was that she didn't force him to begin on an empty stomach. She sent him to the market for bread and melons. To these she added dried figs brought from Castile.

He had just finished carrying in the firewood when Father Olmedo sent for him. Her tightened mouth showed her annoyance but not even Aunt Maria could refuse the summons of a priest. All day Juan trudged happily along the overgrown paths, repeating, *"Huius, huius, huius; huic, huic, huic."* The Latin words had a rhythm that quickened his step.

They returned too early. A chicken was roasting in the fireplace and Aunt Maria made Juan take his father's place at the spit. He turned until his arm ached and his face felt as roasted as the fowl. When they ate, he forgot and threw bones on the floor. Aunt Maria's words completed the scorching of his ears. His father sent him an understanding look but said nothing in his defense.

Juan waited until his aunt left the kitchen. "Don't you think we should go down to the harbor and enlist?"

"No, your aunt is right. You deserve better than I have given you. Look, the place is clean and your stomach full for a change."

"I would rather eat cassava bread in a pigsty."

A scream drowned his father's reply. They rushed to Juan's room. Masses of blue velvet squirmed and wriggled on the dirt floor.

"That dirty, vicious dog," shrieked his aunt. "She's pulled the curtains from the bed. Look here where she's chewed them. Out! Do you hear me, Juan? And she'll never get into this house again."

"Please let her stay. She'll only be here two more days." He couldn't condemn Boba to life with Aunt Maria. He looked accusingly at his father. "I'm sending her on the expedition with Díaz."

Aunt Maria looked from dog to boy. "Very well. She may sleep in here until she goes."

His father reached out a comforting hand, but Juan slipped from under it and turned his back. If only there was some way he could go with Boba. But there wasn't.

During the next two nights he whispered promises into the dog's ears. "You do what Díaz commands. You'll earn shares, and if the voyage is a success we'll have enough money to leave Aunt Maria and live somewhere else. It will be only for a little while. Just a few months and you'll be back."

Too soon it was the last morning. Juan joined the soldiers and sailors at the harbor for mass. As the boats scudded back and forth Juan led Boba to Díaz.

"I wanted to go and instead you take my dog."

The soldier nodded. "I know, Juan, but it may be for the best. The Lord works in mysterious ways."

"Yes, I know. I asked for a miracle and got Aunt Maria."

Mateo came up full of excitement and not the least sorrowful at leave-taking. He hadn't even the decency to stop grinning when the boat carrying Díaz and Boba slipped across the water to the caravel.

He embraced Juan, then said too loudly, "Before I return everyone will know what a crossbow can do." Then he leaped into a loading boat.

Juan turned and met Diego's scornful eyes.

"A nobleman earns his own shares," said the page. "I would never send my dog where I feared to venture."

"And I would hold my tongue about other people's affairs," snapped Juan.

The page flushed. His mouth worked but he turned away before words came. Juan called him back.

"A thousand pardons, Diego. My anger wasn't for you. You just happened to be here. I'm sorry."

Then he turned to watch the ships raise sail and drift from the harbor. Between gusts of wind he could hear Boba howling just as she had done the first time he'd seen her, all trussed for roasting. Juan had never asked where the Indian boys had gotten such a valuable puppy, but from their eagerness to trade her for the three shining buttons left on his doublet Juan was sure they had stolen her. From that moment to this they had not been parted for more than a few moments. The breeze steadied and Juan could hear her no more.

Diego touched his arm gently. "Only six months and she'll return."

Each week seemed a century. Father Olmedo took to his bed with fever. There were no trips to the Indian villages to break the monotony or rescue him from Aunt Maria's endless chores. Often as he carried wood or swept the courtyard he would turn to call Boba before he remembered she was no longer there to answer.

Aunt Maria encouraged Juan's friendship with Diego, and often to escape her sharp tongue he would wander behind the palace to watch the page curry horses or practice with sword and lance. The life of a nobleman's son was not as easy as he'd thought. He formed a grudging admiration for the page as he watched the tumbles and cuts the boy took from his trainers and the dirty menial work he performed as a necessary part of his education. Despite Diego's irritating manners Juan found himself depending more and more on the page's company. The loneliest times were when Diego's duties kept him in the palace.

Juan's father spent most of the time in the forge, often reshaping the same piece of metal several times. When he could find no other refuge Juan would join him. The hammer blows at least drowned out his aunt's voice. As the months of waiting passed, people stopped coming to the forge except on business. The soldiers with their tales of battles kept to the plaza and even the plantation owners didn't linger but unloaded their horses and left quickly.

"The forge is so empty these days there's an echo," said Juan. "What are you making?"

"Hinges and hasps for doors that do not exist," said his father. "There is little work since your Aunt Maria persuaded me to refuse credit. A man cannot dangle his limbs in idleness."

"Perhaps Grijalva's soldiers will return with gold and build fine houses. They will need the hinges then."

Ortega tossed aside his hammer. "If the Grijalva expedition is successful, I could collect all the debts your aunt would not permit the soldiers to make. When I did not demand payment, the forge never cooled and there was always the hope of payment. Now there is nothing. But that is not the worst."

"What could be worse than driving away the soldiers?"

"Your Aunt Maria has taken a fine house on the plaza where she will curry favor with the governor's wife, sisters, cousins, and perhaps his servants as well."

"For what reason?" Juan hoped he and his father were not to move with her.

Ortega glanced at the courtyard before answering. "She claims I haven't received my land because there was no woman to entertain the proper people. By St. James, I earn what I get. I don't wheedle and beg like a nobleman's third son."

Juan kicked at the iron scraps littering the hard-packed dirt floor. He could think of no words to comfort his father.

After a long silence, Ortega said softly, "Perhaps I should have gone with Díaz."

Before Juan could recover from his surprise, someone coughed and a shadow slipped over the scraps at his feet. Diego stood in the doorway.

"A thousand pardons," said the page. "I must hurry back to the palace, but I thought Juan would like to know that one of Grijalva's ships is entering the harbor."

"Only one?" Juan's heart sank. The rest were surely lost. His father had been right not to join. All expeditions were doomed. He crossed himself and prayed the surviving ship was the one Díaz and Boba had boarded.

Chapter Four

LIKE THIEVES IN THE NIGHT

ALL OF Santiago gathered at the harbor. They waited in silence, some crossing themselves, others telling their rosaries. It was an enormous wake, thought Juan. The entire town was already mourning the loss of the men on the other three ships or praying hopelessly for a miracle that would yet save them. Diego pushed his way up beside Juan and stood tugging nervously at his neck ruff.

The first soldiers to go ashore stood up in the small boat, shouting and waving. Their laughing faces, flushed with victory, changed the mood to one of fiesta. The news sped over the harbor.

The expedition had run short of supplies. This ship had returned for help, but the lands to the west were more fabulous than anyone had dreamed. What was more, the natives had been ordered by a great emperor to welcome the Castilians.

Juan craned his neck, too busy to listen to the tales flying around him. Díaz had sailed on Grijalva's ship, but Mateo had gone on this one. The bowman would surely have news of Boba if only Juan could find him. He was beginning to fear the bowman had been lost in battle, when Diego nudged him.

"There he is. He's trying to sneak off to the plaza."

"He just didn't see us," said Juan. "Ho, Mateo!"

The bowman shuffled toward them, embraced each in turn and began talking at full tilt.

"A great success! What did I tell you? Fifteen thousand pesos worth of gold and the others are searching for more. Look at my wounds. Nicked twice on the arm with those black knives the savages use, but my bolts took a heavy toll in spite of what some people say about—"

Diego's voice cut through the speech like a sword. "What happened to Juan's dog?"

Mateo glanced at Juan, then quickly at the harbor. "Why should you think that anything has happened to Boba?"

"Because you babble like a guilty noble brought before the governor."

Juan could read the truth in Mateo's face. Through stiff lips he said, "Boba is dead."

"No, she isn't dead. Not that we know of, at any rate."

"Then you left her wounded and dying."

"We didn't. Upon my honor, she was in perfect health the last time we saw her. Why, she helped us bring down ten deer and a canoeful of rabbits."

Juan's pride in the dog almost erased his grief. "You hear,

Diego? I knew she was a good hunter."

"Well, to be honest, we did a lot of running ourselves to keep her from eating the game alive."

"But what happened to her?"

"You know how dearly that dog loves her stomach. We'd hardly skinned and dressed the game before she was gorging herself. While we were carrying the meat to the boats I saw Díaz ready to push off. I shouted that Boba was feasting on the remains and then went about stowing the meat. I thought Díaz went back for her. He thought I meant I was going to take her aboard our ship."

"You just sailed off and left her?"

"We didn't know. I swear by St. James we didn't. Each of us thought she was on the other's ship. If she'd stopped eating long enough to come to the shore, we'd have put back for her. We didn't know until days later. Then it was too late to turn back to the island for a dog."

"I'll never see her again."

"Yes, you will. She certainly won't starve. Not that dog." Mateo laughed feebly.

"The Indians will eat her."

"There was no sign of Indians on the island. I tell you, she'll be all right."

Unable to bear any more, Juan turned and trudged through the plaza, deaf to the celebration around him. In the bare, swept kitchen Juan poured out the story of his loss. His father listened gravely.

Aunt Maria sniffed loudly. "If you ask me, it's a blessing in disguise. She'll get used to sleeping outdoors. When she gets back, there'll be no more nonsense about having her sleep in the house."

Juan stared at her grim face. "*You* think Boba will be brought back?"

"Why not? That dog isn't going to be stolen. Nobody but you is fool enough to want the beast. The next expedition will find her right where she was left, filthier than ever, no doubt."

"But will there be another expedition? There have been two already and now Governor Velásquez must send relief ships."

"There will be another," said his father. "No Castilian can resist the lure of gold or the promise of an empire."

The relief ships sailed. Days dragged into weeks and still there was no word from the palace. Perhaps the governor had decided against another exploring party. But the royal fifth of the gold brought by Mateo's ship had already been sent to King Charles. The king was sure to order another expedition, for he needed every maravedi for the wars in Europe.

Juan trudged the island with Father Olmedo once again. He hated every tree and puddle for reminding him of times Boba had bounded beside them. Father Olmedo spoke of faith and the power of prayer. Juan clung desperately to both, but each time he saw Diego, the page sadly shook his head. Only Mateo remained unworried. He continued his preparations as if he expected to sail on the next tide.

Ortega helped the young bowman prepare a reserve supply of bolts. One chill rainy day they gathered in the kitchen to feather the last ones. Juan helped his father, keeping the glue hot and holding the feathers carefully in position. Mateo sat near the fire, carefully rubbing beeswax over the string of his crossbow. Aunt Maria had just fussed over sweeping up some dirt he'd made, when Diego burst in without knocking.

"It is done," he announced. "The commander has been named."

From the expression on Diego's face the puddle on the floor might have been tears instead of rain dripping from his cloak.

"When do we sail?" asked Mateo.

"Who is it?" asked Aunt Maria.

"Hernán Cortez," the page said bitterly.

Ortega looked up from the feathers. "The mayor of Santiago?"

"The same."

"It can't be," said Mateo.

Diego's chin lifted haughtily. "Are you suggesting I am not aware of what is occurring in the palace?"

"No, I am suggesting the cursed rain has addled the governor's brains. Why, Cortez has never fought a battle in his life."

"That is true," said Ortega. "Even when he came with us to conquer Cuba he was nothing but Velásquez's secretary. But I would not dismiss him lightly. From the little I have seen and heard, Cortez is a man with the mark of a leader."

Mateo hit his thigh with the crossbow. "A would-be lawyer as commander. And I wanted to go."

"It should have been Porcalla." Mournfully Diego lifted one foot then the other as Aunt Maria mopped about him and hung his dripping cloak near the fire.

Juan glanced at his father. Porcalla, like Velásquez, was a nobleman with many relatives in Cuba. Cortez had the reputation of a rebel, a man who curried favor with no one.

Ortega stroked his beard thoughtfully. "I wonder. Perhaps the governor has made a wise decision."

"Wisdom had nothing to do with it." The page kicked the bench out to give knee room and slumped at the table. "Cortez has been constantly at the governor's side, fawning and pandering, pouring honeyed words into his ear until it turned one's stomach to hear it."

Mateo twanged his bowstring and grinned.

"Even the Instructions have been written as Cortez wants them," continued Diego. "They might just as well read 'Do as you please,' for all the restrictions they set."

"I thought it was to be only another exploration party," said Ortega.

"It will be whatever Cortez decides. The criers have been

ordered to declare shares of gold, silver and slaves to anyone who enlists to conquer and settle the new land."

"Settle?" Ortega leaned forward, his eyes glowing like Mateo's.

"Gold and silver!" shouted the young bowman. "Put my name at the top of the list, Diego. I shall be down tomorrow to make my mark. Who will join me at the wine shop?"

Aunt Maria turned to glare in tight-lipped disapproval. Mateo shrugged good-naturedly and ducked into the misty twilight.

Diego refused Aunt Maria's invitation to dine. "We shall be busy now. My uncle is signing with Cortez. 'Gold is gold,' he says, 'no matter who the commander may be.'"

"Then you'll be going too," said Juan.

"Only as a page, worse luck." He turned at the door to add, "At least you'll be getting your dog back."

But how soon? If the expedition was to settle this new land it might be a year or more before a ship returned to Cuba. Boba might have forgotten him by then. Perhaps she had already. Juan refused to even think that she might be dead.

"Do you think the expedition will stop at that island?" he asked.

"It will stop," said Aunt Maria. "Once I have settled in the new house, I'll have the governor's sisters to visit. A word here and a word there and the next ships out will have orders to search for Boba."

"No!" Ortega's massive fist struck the table. "There will

be no petticoat plots, Maria. I will see to Boba myself. When this expedition leaves I will be with it."

Juan's eyes opened wide. "You mean that?"

His father nodded. "You heard what Diego said. The shares will include land."

"Will you train me in the use of the crossbow?"

His aunt's voice dashed his joy. "You are not going, Juanito. You will stay here with me."

"But even Diego is going."

"Diego is a page," said his father. "You have no training. There is no place for you in the expedition."

"Then I will find a place."

He rushed from the house to hide his tears of disappointment. For lack of other shelter he wandered into the forge. The words had come easily. If only learning to be a soldier were that simple. But Juan knew from watching Mateo and Diego that training with crossbow or sword took more time than he had.

Awkwardly he wielded a broken sword he found in a corner. He pictured himself charging into a horde of screaming Indians, Boba racing beside his horse. Only he was not a swordsman. Boba was still somewhere to the west, alone on an island, and Juan hadn't the faintest notion how he would ever find a way to join the expedition.

"But I will," he said grimly. "By God and St. James, I will find some way to sail with Cortez."

Two days later the banners rose near the harbor—black pendants embroidered in gold with the royal arms, a cross, and a scroll. Juan stood in the midst of the enlisting men and read the words aloud: BROTHERS AND COMPANIONS, FOL-LOW THE CROSS WITH TRUE FAITH AND WE SHALL CONQUER.

"We won't do much conquering if those heathens accept the Cross," said a man at his side.

"What do you mean?" Juan asked.

"The Indians are given three chances to accept the Holy Faith and be baptized. If they don't, then we fight and conquer. But if they take it into their heads to be Christians, then we've got to treat them like royal servants of the king."

"And there goes all the gold and slaves," said another man.

"Don't worry," said the first one. "They always fight. Never seen it otherwise." He winked and jabbed Juan with his elbow. " 'Course the notary always reads it in Castilian, and the language kind of interferes with understanding."

Juan didn't wait to hear more. He ran past the church to Father Olmedo's hut and told the priest what he had heard. "So they don't understand their choice or even about becoming Christians," he finished.

"I know, my son. The treatment of the Indians has been disgraceful, a shame to Castile. We are working to have laws passed for their protection, but everything at court takes time. We do our best while we wait."

"And while you wait these new Indians will be enslaved because they do not understand. Here is a chance to prevent the misery you see here in Cuba."

46

The priest looked thoughtful. "I understand, but there is still the problem of language to overcome."

"Do you remember the two Indians captured on the first expedition? They have learned a little Castilian but not enough to be good translators. Also there has been some question of their loyalty."

Father Olmedo nodded. "But you are loyal."

"Not only loyal but I am already familiar with two Indian tongues. It will be easy for me to learn a third."

The priest's eyes twinkled. "Juan, I fear I must ask you to make a great sacrifice for your God and king. Will you serve me on this expedition now forming?"

"Yes," shouted Juan. "A thousand thanks."

His father agreed more quickly than Juan had expected. The priest would not be taking part in battle. Juan would be as safe as if he were in Santiago. Aunt Maria was not so easily persuaded. She wasted no time arguing with Ortega but went straight to the church. After four visits she announced that she was unable to make Father Olmedo see the light of reason. Grimly she set about preparing Juan's clothes for the journey.

The next weeks were so busy that even the return of the rest of Grijalva's ships was a matter of small importance. The captain's report only confirmed what everyone in Cuba already knew: El Dorado was just over the horizon.

Soon after the ships docked, Díaz tramped into the courtyard carrying a large reed mat bundle.

"Ho, Ortega! Juan!" he shouted. "Come into the kitchen. This you must behold with your own eyes."

He bowed awkwardly to Aunt Maria and turned aside her protests at the dirty bundle. "Surely, señora, you do not object to a treasure on your table?"

"Treasure?" Juan pushed forward eagerly.

"You will receive the shares I promised, Juanito. You and I will be rich and your father will chew his whiskers in envy." The soldier grinned at Ortega. "Perhaps now you will change your mind about joining expeditions."

"I have already signed under Cortez's banner. Juan is also going."

"Even better." Díaz patted the bundle. "This will prove you haven't made a mistake."

Aunt Maria sniffed. "I hope the bundle is not as full of wind as the man holding it. If the sight of your treasure will blind us, at least tell us what it is."

"Hatchets," Díaz said proudly.

"Your brains are on your boot soles," snapped Aunt Maria. "We have more hatchets than we can use."

For once Juan agreed with her, but the soldier's grin widened.

"Do you think we would trade all we owned for ordinary hatchets? Ortega never beat such hatchets as these on his forge. These are gold, pure gold."

He whipped back the mats and spilled the hatchets onto the table.

48

Juan grabbed the nearest. "But it's green."

"Copper," said Ortega.

"They were gold." Díaz examined one after the other but all were tarnished.

"They would look like gold when polished," said Juan's father. "The whole lot may bring you a bottle of wine with which to console yourself."

Juan cringed at Aunt Maria's harsh laughter but the soldier smiled and slapped Ortega on the back.

"You see how much we need you, old friend. With you along, we shall not make the same mistake again."

For Díaz, like most of Grijalva's soldiers, had also signed under Cortez's banner. Even Juan's father was caught in the urgency to be off, to see for himself this new land. Then Governor Velásquez changed his mind.

Cortez, the governor decided, was not to lead the expedition after all. The honor was to go to one of his relatives.

"I will not go," said Ortega. "It will be Cuba all over again."

Juan argued and pleaded far into the night, but his father refused to change his mind.

"With Cortez there was a chance of fair treatment," he said. "Now there is none."

If his father did not go, neither could Juan. Ortega agreed with Aunt Maria on that. With a sigh Juan blew out the candles and groped his way toward his room.

His father grabbed his arm and said, "Wait."

A faint tap came again at the door. Ortega moved softly toward it.

"Who is it?" he asked.

"Mateo," came a muffled voice.

The bolt rasped as Juan's father opened the door.

"Hurry," said the bowman. "Cortez is sailing in secret tonight before Velásquez can stop him. Everyone is to board immediately."

"There will still be time for Velásquez's faction to warn the governor," said Ortega.

Mateo laughed softly. "Not when Cortez has provided each of the governor's relatives and friends with a private escort. I have more calls to make. Juan, you bring the priest."

Juan helped his father collect crossbow, spare parts, bolts, and a few hand tools from the forge. They were ready so quickly Aunt Maria had no time to issue orders. She looked grim as ever but her cheek was damp against Juan's when he embraced her in farewell. Carrying the bundle of clothes she'd prepared for him, Juan trotted beside his father to the plaza.

The wine shops were shuttered for the night, though light showed beneath some of the doors. Soldiers, alone or in groups, moved past the deserted market stalls, but only the thump of boots on hard packed earth and the clink of chain mail shirts broke the eerie silence of the plaza. Ortega touched Juan's shoulder, then joined the silent men hurrying toward the harbor. Juan sped around the church to Father Olmedo's hut.

The priest shook his head when he heard the summons. "This has an air of deceit."

"Cortez has right on his side," protested Juan. "He has borrowed heavily to invest in this expedition. Should he lose everything so the governor can favor a relative? Furthermore, Velásquez has signed the Instructions. Cortez may leave whenever he wishes."

Without another word Father Olmedo gathered what he required for his holy rites and followed Juan back through the plaza. When they reached the wharf, Juan saw three soldiers hustling Diego and his uncle into a boat. The page's stiff back told plainly what he thought of being escorted like a criminal.

The harbor was busier than Juan had ever seen it, yet it was almost as silent as the plaza. Boats shuttled back and forth, their oars muffled. The rhythmic thud of rolled barrels sounded loud as Ortega's hammer and anvil, and the creak of the loading ropes was like a scream. Juan shivered as they waited for a boat to come from the ship.

A hand plucked at his sleeve and he turned to find old One-Eye grinning at him.

"Have you been loading your cassava bread?" Juan asked in a whisper.

The old merchant ignored the question. "Your father will find land this time, if only enough to bury him in."

"If you wish to tell him so, you're too late. He's already aboard."

"I know. I saw him and I told him, the old fool. But he can take care of himself. It's you I'm here to save."

"I'm going," Juan said firmly.

"Ha!" The old man poked Juan's sack. "You've nothing but clothes in there. Throw them away and take these. They're beads for trading."

Juan tried to refuse but One-Eye insisted.

"You can trade for enough gold to get your father a stall like mine. Land! Ha!"

He placed a small dagger in Juan's hand. Though the handle was worn with age and use, the blade was sharp.

"This has served me well," he said. "I pray you won't need it, but I know you will."

"We already owe you so much. I can't take it."

"Take it. If I keep it I may use it to skin the governor." He embraced Juan. "Take care of my old comrade."

"A thousand thanks."

"Go with God."

Juan stepped into the waiting boat. He was but one of three hundred and fifty soldiers who crept like thieves through the night to board the ships. All was ready for the morning tide.

Just before dawn Father Olmedo sang mass. The sailors were raising the anchor when Governor Velásquez and his soldiers appeared on the wharf.

"My friend," the governor shouted between cupped hands, "is this the way you leave, without saying farewell to me?"

"Forgive me, sir," Cortez shouted back. "But such things must be done rather than thought."

Velásquez ordered his soldiers to take the ships, but he'd arrived too late. The tide had turned and the ten ships sailed triumphantly out of the harbor.

"Just wait," Diego warned Juan. "The governor will stop him yet."

When the fleet reached Trinidad, a small port on the opposite side of Cuba, orders were waiting. Velásquez forbade the expedition to continue. Cortez received the chief magistrate of Trinidad aboard his ship.

"What did I tell you?" said Diego. "This is the end of the expedition."

Juan remembered the night they'd boarded ship and the speech Cortez had made to the men. "As long as Cortez can talk," he said, "the expedition is safe."

"He won't silken-tongue the magistrate. He's one of our relatives."

Mateo laughed. "If the captain can't out-talk a Velásquez, I'll take your duty with the half-hour glass tonight."

Mateo pulled his cloak about him and slept beside Juan on the deck as always while Diego stood his regular watch, turning the glass each half hour. For the fleet was not to be stopped.

They sailed on to Havana, took on the rest of their

supplies, built mangers for the sixteen horses, and recruited another hundred and fifty men. At last on February 10, in the year of Our Lord 1519, the fleet heard mass and sailed away from everything Juan had ever known.

Chapter Five

SPIES

DAY AFTER DAY the fleet sailed westward, the daily monotony broken only by the hot noon meal or quarrels among the idle soldiers. Crowded as they were into the small undecked ships, there was no place a man could be alone to work off his ill humor. Juan was grateful to have something to occupy his own time, though learning this new Indian tongue was more difficult than he'd thought.

Part of the trouble was his worry over Boba. Each day increased the chance that something had happened to her. But most of the difficulty lay with the two natives. They sat sullenly against the rail and seemed to begrudge each word Juan coaxed forth. From their sly glances and smiles Juan suspected that the meanings were not always what the Indians claimed, but he had no way of proving it. When land was sighted, he crossed himself and breathed a prayer of thanksgiving.

Rising beyond the beach was one of the great stone pyramids. Birds circled and called. The smell of land rode the breeze. Juan breathed deeply and gazed longingly but he never set foot ashore at Cozumel.

Cortez ordered Escobar's ship to seek a place where they could settle and Juan begged permission to sail with it. He could not enjoy the marvels of this new land until he knew for certain what had happened to Boba. Was the dog still alive? Would she come at his call or had she become wild these past months? For three days he hung over the rail peering at the shore and asking the pilot over and over, "Is this the place?" or "How much farther?"

When they reached the island Juan's heart thudded with fear. From the look of the sand dunes the island was deserted. Yet hadn't Mateo said they'd run down deer and rabbits? There must be low-lying forests beyond the dunes. Impatiently Juan helped load the water casks into the small boat. Halfway to shore he cupped his hands around his mouth and called.

"There." A sailor pointed. "On that dune."

Juan shaded his eyes. "I see nothing."

"I am certain something moved."

"Grass in the wind," said Escobar.

Juan tried again. "Boba! Come, girl."

A dark head rose above the dune. With a yelp the dog raced to the beach. Juan slipped over the side of the boat and waded the last steps. Boba leaped to meet him, whipping her tail and splashing as she jumped to lick his face.

"She's alive," Juan cried.

"And twice the size she was when we left her," said the pilot. "There can't be a rabbit left on this island."

Juan nodded. Boba looked better fed than he'd ever seen her. Had she hunted or had she discovered some Indian village to raid? What had she seen and done in this new land? Juan hugged her, burying his face in the sleek fur that was no longer loose and flabby.

"It doesn't matter," he murmured. "You're safe."

Perhaps safer here on the island than with the expedition. For a moment he wondered if it was best to take her back to the army, but he couldn't bear to leave her. Boba must have feared he would. She never left his side until they had filled the casks and were safely on board the ship.

Escobar sailed farther along the coast, and chose a townsite for Cortez at a place the Grijalva expedition had named San Juan de Ulúa. They turned back, sailing only as far as Tabasco, where they found the fleet anchored in the mouth of the river. Cortez must have landed days ago, for all the men and horses were ashore. As they approached the camp Boba's nose quivered and she licked her chops. Juan's own mouth watered at the smell of roasting fish and chicken. He held the dog close as they walked through the camp. He needed no one to tell him there'd been a battle. There were wounded at every campfire. Juan's father limped from an arrow wound in the thigh and the livid red cut across Mateo's jawbone promised another scar for the bowman to boast of.

Ortega embraced Juan with a relieved sigh. "I feared Indians had also attacked the ship."

"We did not land near villages. But tell me what has happened here."

His father pushed him down beside the fire. "Eat first. On campaigns, there is always time for talk but food like this is rare."

"Greetings," called Mateo. "Forgive me for not embracing you, but I must fortify my position and prepare to repel the enemy. Down, you four-legged stomach!"

The young bowman sat on the ground, the space between his spread legs filled with mats piled high with strange fruit, chickens, and large round flat cakes. With one arm he parried Boba's assaults, with the other he piled more reed mats over the food. Boba settled on the ground, head resting on Mateo's leg, her nose against the protecting mats.

"You can lie there until you turn to stone," he grumbled. "You get no food from me."

Boba's eyes rolled toward his. Her tail thumped. The bowman sighed.

"One tortilla then." But he drew two of the large cakes from beneath the mats and broke them apart to keep the dog from swallowing them whole. Ortega removed a chicken from the spit and shared it with his son.

"What of the battle?" Juan asked between mouthfuls.

"A mere skirmish," said Mateo. "Only three hundred Indians to each one of us."

Juan turned to his father. "That can't be true."

"It is. The plains were covered with Indians and they are nothing like the ones in Cuba. These are trained soldiers, equal to any in Europe."

Tabasco was a large town and only one of many. How many thousands of soldiers were there to fight the few hundred in this camp?

"They were no match for us," said Mateo. "We made them show their heels."

"No thanks to you." Diego stepped into the firelight and greeted Juan. "I heard you'd returned with the dog. Is she well?"

He bent over the greyhound, frowning at her quivering muscles. Mateo pulled out a chicken leg and jabbed it into the dog's mouth. She stopped trembling.

"Of course she's well." Mateo scowled at the page. "You think we starve her? And what did you mean, no thanks to me?"

"Simply that you had nothing to do with routing the Indians. It was the horses that put them to flight. Is that not so, Ortega?"

Juan's father nodded. "They believe the horses are gods of some kind. When Cortez led the horsemen in a charge the Indians fled."

"And who faced their arrows and black swords while Cortez circled the swamp?" demanded Mateo.

"The swordsmen," said Diego.

"Swordsmen, eh?" He fingered the welt on his face. "I suppose you think the barber gave me this."

"No, I don't believe you'd get that close to sharp steel." Not waiting for the fuming bowman to reply, Diego turned to Juan. "Have you heard what that lawyer has done?"

"You mean Cortez?"

"The same. He has taken possession of this land in the name of King Charles."

Mateo snorted. "I suppose you think he should have claimed it for Velásquez."

"That would be treason," said Juan.

"Which would suit this popinjay's uncle and his friends. They're hopping like fleas on hot coals for fear their cousin Velásquez will lose out on a little gold or glory."

"What about the governor's money?" said Diego. "Is that not to be returned?"

"And what about Cortez?" countered the bowman. "I heard he went into debt for this expedition."

"Without Governor Velásquez there would be no expedition."

They were shouting now. To distract them Juan seized on the first subject his eyes discovered.

"Is that a bandage on your wrist, Diego?"

"Just a scratch from cleaning my uncle's sword."

"Ha! His uncle caught him sampling the wines," said Mateo.

"That's a lie and an insult." Diego reached for the short sword at his side.

60

"Would the great don attack an unarmed man?" Mateo spread wide his arms in a gesture of helplessness. Immediately Boba scratched aside the reed mats, dove into the unprotected food, and snapped what came first to her jaws. Everyone leaped to the rescue. When the yelling was over and the salvaged bits of food repacked in the mats, page and bowman had forgotten their quarrel. Ortega surveyed their depleted supplies.

"You will have to tie that dog or she will have the rest before the night is out."

"Won't you raid tomorrow?" asked Juan.

His father shook his head. "There is no raiding when you serve with Cortez. He had soldiers whipped at Cozumel for taking chickens and gold from the village."

Juan wondered if Father Olmedo had anything to do with this policy of fair treatment. He gestured to the cookfires. "But all this food."

"Brought by the Indians after we put them to rout. They would never have attacked us in the first place if it hadn't been for a traitor."

Before leaving Cozumel, Cortez had heard of two Castilians among the Indians, survivors of an ill-fated expedition to Darien eight years ago. One had become a chieftain and refused to meet the expedition. It was he who had urged the Indians to attack. The other had joined Cortez and was acting as interpreter.

"A good thing, too," Ortega added. "Those two who were teaching you deserted during the battle."

Mateo chuckled. "Hung their good Castilian clothes on a tree limb and took to the woods."

The most important news was of the peace offerings brought by the Indians the day before. Besides food and gold they'd brought twenty slaves. Among them was a princess from Mexico, the great city from which all the gold was said to come. She'd been baptized by Father Olmedo and given the name Marina. But she was always courteously addressed as Doña Marina, for her soft voice and gracious manner were equal to that of any Castilian lady of royal blood.

The princess spoke the tongues of Mexico and Tabasco. Aguilar, the survivor of Darien, spoke Castilian and the language of Tabasco. Through both of them Cortez would be able to communicate with the people of Mexico, but it would be easier if Doña Marina would learn Castilian. Father Olmedo asked Juan if he would help Aguilar teach her, at the same time learning her tongue. Juan agreed.

On Palm Sunday they heard mass and boarded the ships for Ulúa. Juan once again began lessons. They were frequently interrupted by Mateo or Díaz pointing out places of interest. A river, snow-capped mountains, a white island, and then another where the tops of pyramids loomed over the foliage.

"The Isle of Sacrifices," Mateo said grimly.

Juan and Diego leaned on the rail beside him, staring in horrified fascination.

"Is it true?" Juan asked at last.

Diego shrugged. "Their temples at Cozumel and Tabasco were smeared with blood, but it could have been from animals."

"It wasn't," said Mateo. "I could tell you . . . but one must see for one's self to believe it."

Juan couldn't believe the stories of human sacrifice. He'd spent hours with Doña Marina and she fully deserved the title of Castilian royalty. Juan could not imagine anyone so gentle and kind worshiping idols that demanded human blood.

The afternoon of Holy Thursday they anchored off Ulúa. Two canoes made of hollowed logs, fully as large as Díaz had said, came to meet them. Juan stood by as Aguilar translated, for the tongue was that of Tabasco. The local cacique welcomed them and promised to provide for their needs. Cortez thanked the cacique and presented the Indian ruler and his followers with beads and other trifles. But the next morning, even before mass was said, Cortez ordered the cannons taken ashore and mounted on the highest dunes. Then an altar was built and Father Olmedo sang mass, celebrating Good Friday in the new land.

The men were building huts when the Indians returned. Ortega reached for his crossbow with one hand and pushed Juan to the ground with the other.

"Stay here," he ordered, and ran with the rest of the soldiers.

Juan lay tensed for action. He felt for One-Eye's knife,

63

now safely sheathed in leather and hidden inside his waist-band. His father thought him too young for weapons. But what if the Indians broke through the line of soldiers and came at him? He listened but there were no sounds of fighting. He looked over at Boba. The dog appeard interested in what was happening beyond the dunes but she wasn't bristling with alarm. Her ears pricked forward and her nose quivered. Juan stood up. Dozens of Indians were scattering through the camp but they carried food instead of arms.

With a firm grip on the dog's new leather collar Juan strolled over to join the soldiers. He watched in amazement as the mats were spread on the ground to receive gifts from Montezuma, emperor of Mexico. The first was a headdress of feathers long enough to hang to a man's waist, all studded with gold stars. Then came a mask with features more nightmarish than those of García, the scarred swordsman everyone agreed was the ugliest man in camp, if not in creation. Juan smiled at the jokes passed around at García's expense, then gasped as a tall headdress of jaguar hide was laid beside the other two headpieces. Attached to the jaguar hide was a cloak woven of feathers, brilliant lustrous feathers worn by no bird Juan had ever seen. What strange creatures roamed this land? And who were these people who wove feathers into intricate designs?

Green gems, figures of gold, and other curious objects too small for Juan to see clearly were laid beside the three headdresses. Then the cacique stepped back and waited expectantly. His shoulders dropped slightly, as if in disappointment, when Cortez began to speak.

Cortez, through Aguilar, thanked him in the name of the great cacique, King Charles, whom he served. A murmur of protest rose from some of the soldiers.

"What of our cousin Velásquez?" muttered one.

Cortez continued as if he'd heard nothing. In the name of King Charles he presented gifts for the Emperor Montezuma. Beads, gems and a carved armchair.

"This chair is for the emperor to use when we meet," he told Aguilar. "Ask when that will be."

"You have just arrived and already you want to meet Emperor Montezuma," replied the cacique.

Even if he hadn't understood the language, Juan would have known that the Indian was displeased about something. He missed the rest of the conference, for he realized Boba was no longer at his side. He caught a glimpse of her thin tail disappearing behind the delegation of Indians. Juan followed. His suspicions were correct. Boba had sniffed out the Indians' food supply. As he hauled her away he noticed an Indian crouched on the side of a dune. A long white paper was spread before him. He seemed to be writing with a brush.

Hand tight on Boba's collar, Juan went to look over the Indian's shoulder. He caught his breath in amazement. It was not writing but pictures. There in detail were the ships, the men with swords and crossbows, and a figure that was a perfect likeness of Cortez himself. More important were clusters and groupings that could only be a counting of their numbers. Though the artist had paid him no attention, Juan backed carefully away. Then he turned and ran to find Díaz.

"They are spies," he told the soldier. "They are drawing a full report to send back to the emperor."

As Díaz hurried to tell Cortez Juan glanced over the camp. There were fewer than five hundred men, thirty-two of them armed with crossbows and thirteen with the unreliable arquebuses, sixteen horses, and four small cannon. Was this enough to conquer an empire where one province alone had been able to muster three hundred soldiers to each Castilian? True, they had won at Tabasco, but only because the Indian had feared the unknown horses.

Cortez must have remembered that also, for he had the men with horses mount and gallop up and down the beach. Then the arquebusiers discharged their weapons and the cannon were fired into the air. Juan grinned as he thought of the artist on the dune. He wondered if he still painted or if, like the rest, he'd retreated from the fearful weapons. Not until Díaz visited their hut that night did Juan, his father, and Mateo discover the most important event of the visit.

"The cacique asked if he could borrow García's old helmet," said the soldier. "He said it looks very much like the one worn by their god Quetzalcoatl. He wants their priests in Mexico to compare it with the ancient drawings."

Ortega frowned. "Surely they don't believe García is a god."

"He's as ugly as one of their idols," said Mateo. "He could wear that mask presented today and not one of us would notice."

The men laughed but Juan wondered if his father's guess wasn't close to the truth. He must ask Doña Marina about this Quetzalcoatl.

"But wait," said Díaz. "You haven't heard the best. Our commander told the cacique he was welcome to the helmet, but would he return it full of gold dust, as we'd like to compare the quality of their gold with that from our own land."

"There can't be that much gold dust in the world," said Mateo.

The cacique not only returned the helmet filled to the neck with gold dust, he also presented Cortez with a gold disk as large as a cartwheel and another just as large of silver. Both were skillfully worked with strange intricate designs.

"All that gold," said Mateo that night. "Just handed it over as if it were a pitcher of water."

"Did you ever see anything as beautiful as those disks?" said Juan. "I wonder how they do it."

"I wonder how much more is left in that Mexico."

Juan thought of the trading beads One-Eye had given

him. How much gold would they bring? He slapped at a mosquito and moved away from the firelight, hoping to lose the swarm.

Mateo held out a foot. "Don't they have a god who wears cracked leather boots? I'd be happy to let the Indians borrow them on the same terms as they took the helmet." He straightened, eyes glinting with excitement.

"By heaven, that's what I'm going to do. I'm going to fill my boots with gold. What about you, Ortega?"

"My boots are already well filled."

The young bowman looked puzzled. "But you have nothing in your boots."

"I have my feet. They will support me in my old age far better than the gold you chase and will never capture. I'll save my boots to walk my land."

"Ha! With a bootful of gold I can buy the whole island of Cuba."

"Remember that one fifth of that gold must go to King Charles."

Mateo laughed. "The king is a long way off."

The next day he had Juan help him trade for a pair of native sandals. Then the bowman tied his boot tops together with thongs and wore them hanging from his belt. They swung and thumped awkwardly against his thigh, but Mateo seemed not to notice. He was too busy trying to fill them with gold. Juan thought of the beads in his bundle of clothes and decided to do some trading of his own.

Most of the men bartered with the local Indians, giving beads for small ornaments and figures of gold. Some of the gold they then traded to the sailors for fresh fish. Though the Indians brought tortillas and chickens to the camp, they could not feed the entire army. The salt pork and cassava bread brought from Cuba were almost at an end. Without the Indians and sailors there would have been empty stomachs in camp. As it was, no one overate but no one complained. There was food enough, no fighting, and plenty of gold for trading. Despite the voracious mosquitoes the men were content.

Another delegation from Montezuma was welcomed. The Indians presented more gifts, burned incense around Cortez, and chanted for hours. After their ceremony ended, Father Olmedo with Juan's help explained the true faith to the Indians. They listened politely but turned away unbaptized. Only Father Olmedo was disappointed with the expedition's progress.

The men sang and joked around the fires that night. Estimates of Mexico's wealth grew at each telling. They fell asleep confident that God and St. James had smiled upon the men of Castile. They woke to the first of many days when no one smiled.

Chapter Six

MAROONED

THE INDIANS WERE GONE. Not just the delegation from Mexico but every Indian from the nearby villages. It could mean nothing or much, but the soldiers had a more important problem to argue over. Governor Velásquez's friends and relatives chose that day to demand that all gold be turned over to the expedition's treasurer. Soldiers, they said, had no right to trade privately. Everything belonged to the expedition except the royal fifth that went to King Charles. Cortez objected but the Velásquez faction had their way.

The soldiers lined up and sullenly dumped their gold at the treasurer's feet. Juan wished he'd saved his trade beads for the uncertain future. Not because he was losing a few golden clasps. With the gold portioned equally, Juan was certain to receive more than he'd placed on the golden heap. But it would be at the expense of Mateo and others who had traded heavily. It wasn't fair and Juan felt guilty even though he was not at fault.

"I had one foot nearly filled," said Mateo as he pulled his boots back on his feet. "What right have those sons of baboons to take our gold?"

"We still have shares in the expedition," Juan reminded him. "The gold collected will be counted in those."

"A fat lot of good that does me. After the royal fifth is taken and the captains grab their share, there won't be enough left for the rest of us to replace my bowstring. It's out-and-out thievery. Even Cortez said it wasn't fair."

Ortega smiled at his grumbling but said nothing. Mateo scowled.

"You needn't sit there gloating. Your land has gone the same way as my gold."

"What do you mean?"

Now Mateo smiled. "Haven't you heard? Now that the Velásquez party has collected the gold for the governor they want to return to Cuba."

"They can't. Cortez said we were to conquer and *settle*."

"The official charter says nothing about settling, just trade. The commander must obey it and return to Cuba."

Diego chose that moment to look into the hut.

"Get out of here, you two-legged insect," shouted Mateo. "Go back to your cutpurse uncle and his friends."

"But I have orders from the commander."

"Get out!" Mateo hurled a sandal at the page. Juan scrambled to his feet, but before he could follow Diego there was scuffling and muted voices outside the hut. Again a figure blocked the doorway. Mateo grabbed the other sandal, but it was Díaz who ducked into the hut.

"Is it true we're to sail for Cuba?" asked Ortega.

Díaz nodded. "Didn't that page give you the orders to board ship?"

"I won't go. By Job's boils, I came to settle and I'll settle if I must live among the Indians as Aguilar did."

Mateo snorted. "Now who's the fool?"

"Not my father." Juan glared at the bowman.

"Peace, my friends. We may still outwit Velásquez." Quickly Díaz outlined the plan. Tomorrow they would all gather and demand that Cortez found a city by drawing up a charter and electing a town council. Once the charter was signed the expedition became a legal Castilian city responsible only to King Charles. Even if Velásquez appeared in person, his orders would have no authority.

"But we must demand the city publicly so the notary can record that Cortez was obeying the will of his men."

"I want no part of any city founded in this pesthole," said Mateo. "The mosquitoes are big enough to bring down with the crossbow."

"It doesn't matter where we actually found the city so long as we draw up the charter tomorrow and break our ties with Velásquez."

Ortega frowned. "I've been counting. There aren't enough of us. It can't be done without the support of some of the Velásquez party."

Díaz sighed. "That's the worm in the apple. Cortez is certain he can manage most of them, but for a price."

"Our gold," guessed Mateo. "I knew it would end in the captains' purses instead of in the expedition's profits for shares."

"Part of it. The gold dust from the helmet will sweeten some of the Velásquez tempers, but in return Cortez wants a fifth of all treasure."

"That is fair," said Ortega. "For if there is any blame cast it will fall on his head. I agree."

"I don't," said Mateo. "The royal fifth and then the Cortez fifth. That's almost half bitten out before any shares are figured."

Juan grinned. "And what is left after they remove forty per cent of all the gold in Mexico? Your share will be only enough to fill ten pairs of boots. You'll be a poor bowman indeed, Mateo."

"Mexico?" The bowman looked puzzled then his face cleared. "That's right! If we found the city, we'll stay and march on Mexico."

"Then you agree?"

"Of course. I'm no fool."

"Good." Díaz rose stiffly. "You can all help pass the word through the camp, but be sure no Velásquez men hear of the plan."

As they moved out Juan noticed that Mateo had suddenly developed a limp.

"Mateo," he whispered, "are you sure you emptied that right boot for the treasurer?"

The bowman grinned. "A good soldier always holds something in reserve for emergencies. I only wish these boots were a bit overlong."

Juan helped his father recruit the bowmen and Cortez took care of the captains. The city of Vera Cruz was founded on paper, with Cortez elected captain and chief justice. All ties were legally cut with Governor Velásquez.

But a new enemy invaded their camp: hunger.

The salt pork was finished. The remaining cassava bread crawled with worms and weevils. Only Boba ate it with relish. But that too was soon gone. Without the Indians to help with tortillas and chickens the few fish caught were only tantalizing morsels. The men hunted but even the shore birds had fled to safer beaches. Mateo greeted each hungry morning by calling down a variety of curses upon the heads of the vanished Indians. He had just finished wishing a horrible disfigurement on all their descendants when Diego burst into the hut.

He sputtered and choked over his words, then threw the leather strips he held at Juan. The action released his voice. He pointed a trembling finger at Boba.

"That stupid, useless animal chewed my uncle's horse trappings to pieces."

Juan looked from the tattered leather to the dog lying beside him. The greyhound rolled over on her back and thumped her tail.

74

"How do you know it was Boba?"

"Who else would eat it?"

Mateo reached for the leather and inspected it thoughtfully. "I might, providing it's well salted."

"It was that monster. I saw her slinking away." Diego sank to the mats as if the shouting had exhausted him. He covered his face with shaking hands. "It will take me days to mend it."

"I'll keep her tied from now on," Juan promised. Boba had come in just a few moments before Diego, but she often roamed the camp before dawn. "We'll help you mend it, too."

Mateo opened his mouth to protest, but Juan glared him into grumbling consent. "Diego will help us dig shellfish in return."

As the three worked on the beach they discussed possible reasons for the Indians' desertion.

"They're afraid to fight us, so they're starving us out," said Mateo.

"Doña Marina said the priests must have decided that Cortez is not their god Quetzalcoatl." Juan had already told them the tale of the fair god who had vanished across the sea, promising to return this very year. "They have been suspicious ever since Cortez failed to select Quetzalcoatl's headdress from the three offered."

Mateo straightened and wiped his face. "If they know we're men, why don't they attack and get it over with?"

"Doña Marina doesn't know."

"Then I was right. They're afraid."

"I pray that you are right," said Diego. "We are in no condition to defend ourselves."

Mateo hotly denied the possibility of defeat, but before an argument could develop Díaz called from his guard post up the beach. Juan shaded his eyes.

"Indians. Five of them."

Mateo cursed. "I'll never leave my crossbow in camp again."

"From the way Díaz is waving they must be messengers. Come."

When they were nearer they could see the five Indians were different from any they'd met so far. Not only were their cloaks woven in a different pattern, but they wore blue stones forced into holes cut in their ears and lower lips.

"See what you can make of their talk," said Díaz. "I've never heard it before."

The Indians spoke again. Juan fought a desire to cheer.

"They speak Nahuatl, the language of Mexico."

"Then ask them why their precious Montezuma is letting us starve on the beach," growled Mateo.

The emperor's name brought another flurry of speech from the Indians. Juan shook his head.

"We must take them to Doña Marina. I'm not sure I understand. It seems their cacique is tired of paying taxes to Montezuma. He has heard we are great warriors and would like us to visit him."

Mateo laughed gleefully. "An invitation to a revolution."

He slapped the page on the shoulder. "You may get that stickpin of yours bloodied yet, Diego."

"I may be wrong," Juan warned. But Doña Marina confirmed his translation. The cacique of Cempoala was tired of sending his best cloth, mats and gems to Mexico. His heart despaired at having his finest young men and women taken to the great city for sacrifice in the temples.

"God has sent us to help these people," said Father Olmedo.

Cortez agreed. So far, the city of Vera Cruz was nothing but a legal charter, a paper city. After consulting with men who had been on the other expeditions, Cortez decided to actually found the real city of Vera Cruz near Cempoala in the land of Montezuma's enemies. The ships sailed to the chosen site while the army marched for Cempoala.

The first night they made a hungry, cheerless camp. The next day Cortez sent out foraging parties from both sides of the line of march. Mateo borrowed Boba to help hunt, for Father Olmedo thought it most important for Juan to walk with Doña Marina and complete his study of Nahuatl. The knowledge that Diego was a member of one of the foraging parties while he stayed behind spoiled any pleasure Juan might have taken in the Indian princess's company. It seemed he was doomed to miss all the excitement.

That night they dined on ripe plums and chicken. Juan watched eagerly as the meat was portioned, one small piece for each.

"I thought Cortez ordered nothing to be taken from the

villages even if they were deserted," said Ortega.

Mateo put on an exaggerated expression of horror. "Do you think I'd disobey my commander?"

"Then how did you get the chickens?" Juan had the strange feeling he'd taken Diego's place. That was the sort of questioning the page usually did, but tonight Diego sat listlessly staring into the small fire. His uncle was on guard duty, so he'd brought them plums and accepted an invitation to share the chicken. He didn't even lift his head as Mateo gave his version of chicken stealing.

"On my honor, the chickens were not taken from the village. Boba and I strolled about the buildings. When we left we discovered all these chickens had run squawking into the forest. We couldn't leave them for some wild animal, could we?"

Juan noticed Mateo was wearing sandals again, but since he was sharing stolen chicken Juan didn't feel he had a right to ask if the boots hanging from the bowman's belt had toes full of gold. Between mouthfuls he glanced around the fire. Diego sat staring at the chicken leg in his hands.

"What's the matter, Diego?"

The page handed him the piece of chicken. "I'll just eat plums. I haven't much appetite for meat tonight, especially legs."

Mateo stopped chewing to search the page's face. He grunted. "You'll get used to it."

"To what?" asked Juan.

"Ask him. I'd say he was in one of their temples today."

Juan stared at the white-faced page. "Then it's true."

"No, you don't know half the truth. Boys with their chests torn open and their hearts taken out. Then they eat—" The page clapped a hand over his mouth and bolted into the darkness.

Juan stared at the meat in his hands. His stomach churned. Quickly he passed it over to Mateo. The bowman snorted.

"Fine soldiers you two will make. You think you slay enemies by spitting at them?"

"It's different in battle."

The bowman shrugged. "Blood is blood."

But Juan noticed Boba was soon growling happily over the chicken.

"She helped catch it," said Mateo. "She's entitled to a share."

"I didn't say anything."

"Well, don't." He picked up his crossbow. "Time to change the guard, Ortega."

The next day Juan again marched beside Doña Marina. The Indian princess had devised a simple way to teach Castilian to herself and Nahuatl to Juan. They asked each other questions, repeating questions and answers in both tongues. Doña Marina was curious about Cortez and the land from which he'd come. Juan had endless questions about every plant, bird, and animal he saw. There were other questions, questions he wondered if he dared ask as they passed through many villages, all deserted, though fresh sacrifices dripped on the altars. The stench of the blood-caked temples was enough to sicken Juan without the added horror of the mutilated bodies. He could hold his questions no longer.

"Why?" he asked Doña Marina. "Why do they do this?"

"They are afraid. They search in the hearts for signs of the future."

"Couldn't they search in a goat's heart?"

"Goat?" She frowned over the strange word.

"Any animal."

"No, the gods will accept only human blood." She smiled at his expression. "You must understand. We have been taught that only human blood keeps the sun in the sky and the corn growing. It is a terrible thing to know your children may climb those steps, but dare you say 'no' and risk destroying the world?"

"But the world wouldn't end."

"I know that now. Soon others will know."

But Juan wondered uneasily if the Indian priests didn't possess some sort of strange power. The deserted villages must mean the signs had been bad, and certainly these bloodthirsty gods would have no future if the Castilians had their way.

The land became greener. Water was plentiful and the growth dense and flowering. Cortez sent scouts ahead to warn Cempoala of the army's approach. They marched through cultivated fields and flowering orchards. Ortega's step quickened and his eyes brightened. There had been no such farms in Cuba. The town before them was large as any in Castile.

"It looks like Seville," said Ortega. "Look, isn't that like the house of the Duke of Medina?"

The Cempoalans came to greet them with bouquets of flowers. The cacique sent his regrets, but he was unable to leave the city. When Juan saw him, he understood. The cacique was the fattest man he'd ever seen. What was more, he was not selfish about the food he evidently loved himself. For the first time in many weeks the men of Castile slept with full stomachs.

The next days Father Olmedo kept Juan busy explaining the word of God. The Cempoalans listened eagerly and many were baptized, but the fat cacique still refused Cortez's demand to destroy the old gods. One afternoon the commander led fifty soldiers across the plaza and climbed the tallest pyramid. When Juan realized what was going to happen, he rushed to find Father Olmedo.

"You must stop him, Father. These people may turn on us."

The priest hitched up his cassock and ran with Juan to the square. It was too late. Stone idols were already crashing down the steep steps. The Cempoalans wailed and hid their faces. When the last idol shattered, the Indians fled to their homes and silence fell over the city.

Father Olmedo met Cortez at the foot of the temple steps.

81

"This is not the way." The priest's voice was strained with anger. "All men will fight to the death for three things: their children, their land, and their gods."

"Then we shall gladly die for the true God," replied Cortez. "Though I have been told the Cempoalans will not fight but will extinguish their fires and wait for the world to end."

"It is still wrong. I beg you, Hernán, remember the Romans. They let the conquered keep their gods."

"Is a man of God suggesting I leave these heathens to worship idols? That I turn my head while they feed their gods on human hearts?"

"I am suggesting it is better for the Indians to smash the idols themselves. Only then will we be sure they are true to the Holy Faith."

"Far simpler to show them that their false gods have no power." The commander turned and climbed over the pile of rubble.

Father Olmedo shook his head. "God grant that he learn there are some things better thought than done. Come, Juan. We must pray."

After Evensong, orders were issued for all to sleep in their sandals with weapons at hand. Juan dozed fitfully, waking at every footstep and sword clank. But there was no attack.

All the next day and night the Indians crouched in their homes waiting for the end. But the sun rose and shone as before. The birds sang. The corn stood high in the fields.

Their hearts still beat. One by one the Cempoalans came forth to touch their heads three times to the ground before Cortez and Father Olmedo.

The temple was cleaned and whitewashed. An altar was erected and a cross raised. The Indian priests cut their blood-caked hair and took over the care of the altar. The Cempoalans rejoiced, but the spirit of freedom was short lived.

Into the city strutted five men in richly feathered cloaks. In one hand they carried staffs of office and in the other bouquets that they sniffed as if the common air was unfit for their nostrils. Beside them ran servants with feathered fans to whisk away flies.

The fat cacique trembled and wrung his hands. "Montezuma's tax collectors. What shall I do?"

"Put them in chains," replied Cortez.

The cacique was speechless at the thought. Father Olmedo called Juan to his side.

"Remind him that we destroyed his idols and the world is still here. Our Lord will protect him as well against Montezuma."

Cortez added his words of persuasion. The cacique wavered, then decided. The tax collectors were arrested.

"And if that doesn't knock old Montezuma off his throne, I miss my guess," said Mateo. His eyes took on a faraway look as he patted the boots hanging at his side.

Ortega shook his head. "It isn't like Cortez to deliberately seek trouble with Montezuma. I don't understand it."

83

The next morning two of the prisoners were missing. Diego swore Cortez had released them to carry tales to Mexico, but the commander made a great show of anger. He told the cacique he would take the other three with him and put them on the ships in chains to be sure they didn't escape. The cacique quickly agreed it was best. He gave them porters to carry their supplies and food to last them to the coast.

Ortega chuckled. "Cortez is a lawyer who takes both sides of the case."

"Do you think he set the tax collectors free?" asked Juan.

"I'm sure of it. Cortez is no fool. He wants to enter Mexico peacefully, but if he can't, he has all the soldiers in this province to help fight. The fat one has no choice, since he arrested the tax collectors. But our commander rescued them, or so he will tell Montezuma." He gazed about wistfully. "I would be content right here in Cempoala."

"Then why don't we just settle in Vera Cruz and be done with campaigning?"

"I must earn my land first. Besides, you heard what the fat one said. Every tribe in this land pays tribute to Montezuma. They shake in terror at the name. We'd be fools to settle here before the power of Mexico is broken."

In the weeks after they met the ships Juan discovered the meaning of hard labor. He'd thought Aunt Maria overworked him but as he dug dirt, hauled it, mixed it for bricks, and then lugged the bricks to build church, jail and living quarters, he began to think of his aunt almost wistfully. Cortez drove the men to the limit of their strength to finish the town. No one dared complain, for the commander sweated under loads of dirt and laid bricks with the rest.

Hunting parties and Indians kept them well supplied with food but Juan was too tired to eat. Boba no longer begged for a share of his supper. She waited until he fell asleep and then helped herself. Many a soldier awoke to discover his food had disappeared while he dozed.

The work was regularly interrupted by delegations from Montezuma. The first one thanked Cortez for releasing the tax collectors (the last three had been sent back to Mexico as soon as Cortez left Cempoala), but Montezuma complained of the Castilians' associating with dishonest people who refused to pay their taxes. Cortez replied that he would be happy to come to Mexico and explain his actions. The next delegation came laden with gold to soften Montezuma's regrets that he could not entertain the Castilians in Mexico. The more Cortez insisted on marching to Mexico, the greater grew the gifts and the weaker the excuses for Montezuma's refusal to see them.

"We're being richly paid to stay away," said Mateo.

He and Juan had just finished tiling a roof and were resting in the shade of the building.

"It can't be that he's afraid of us," said Juan. "From what the Indians say he can call on thousands of warriors."

"I'm not going to worry over the reason. A few more

threats and I'll be able to fill my boots without stirring from Vera Cruz."

"Greetings." Diego dropped down beside them. He held out a pineapple, a fruit Juan hadn't yet acquired a taste for. "I thought you might like to share this."

Mateo eyed him suspiciously. "Why?"

"Because we are friends." Diego drew his dress sword and sliced the fruit. Mateo ate eagerly. Juan accepted one piece out of courtesy but refused any more.

"Juan is right," said Diego. "Montezuma can destroy us as easily as one steps on a spider."

"Not while we have our cannon mounted and the Cempoalans to fight with us."

"Exactly." The page leaned forward. "But what happens if we march inland? We'll be surrounded by tribes under Montezuma's rule. They can attack from all sides. There will be no way out."

Juan shivered at the picture. Mateo's face darkened.

"There's truth in that." The bowman gazed toward the ships riding at anchor. "Perhaps we should take what we have and leave."

"It would be wise," Diego agreed.

"Then again, if Montezuma can give away so much gold, just think how much more there must still be in Mexico."

"You will never live to see it."

Suddenly Juan saw where the page had been leading

them. He remembered things he'd heard when translating for Father Olmedo when strange Indians wandered into Vera Cruz.

"Cempoala isn't the only province that is tired of Montezuma's taxes," Juan said. "Much of the country we march through will be friendly."

The page agreed it was possible. "But suppose all this assurance of friendship is only bait to lure us into a trap?"

"Then 'Santiago and at them!' God will lend strength to our arms." Mateo rose and signaled to Juan. "We have another roof to tile if we wish to sleep dry tonight."

When they were out of the page's hearing Mateo said, "That pipsqueak's uncle and his friends are up to something again."

"What can they do? Cortez has sent much of the gold with his letters to King Charles. The king is sure to back Cortez."

"Unless Velásquez catches scent of that shipful of gold and learns he's to have no share in it."

"He won't. The ship has orders not to stop at Cuba."

"Ha! Orders. Did you ever know a Castilian who could resist a chance to boast?"

Juan glanced at the horizon, half expecting to see Governor Velásquez's ships coming to place Cortez in irons. But surely the men sent to Castile would not risk losing everything by disobeying orders. He meant to discuss it with his father and Díaz, but they were occupied with other problems. For the first time since they'd arrived at Cempoala the men were restless and grumbling. With each gold-laden delegation from Mexico the feeling grew that they should abandon Vera Cruz and return to Cuba while they could. It was whispered that if Cortez refused to sail, the soldiers would take things into their own hands. Juan only half heard the rumors. He was engaged in a conquest of his own.

Boba's foraging had led Juan to a strange long-nosed animal that snuffled and rooted through the damp undergrowth. It seemed peaceful and not overly timid so long as Juan held Boba firmly in check. Each morning before dawn Juan crept past the guards and followed Boba to the creature's favorite watering spot. By offering food Juan was patiently luring the animal closer to friendship. One morning his efforts were rewarded by the touch of the snout on his outstretched hand before Boba growled and lunged, frightening the anteater back to the thick forest.

"I'll leave you tied in the village tomorrow," Juan threatened, but he was so pleased with his near success in taming a wild creature that he couldn't remain angry with Boba. He raced her to the beach in search of gulls. Boba took up the chase but Juan paused, searching the sky. There was something missing. The pale sky was clear. Where were the ships? The masts at least should be visible from where he stood.

With Boba beside him he clambered to the top of a dune. From there he saw the masts, crazily tilted masts, dipping slowly toward the surface of the sea. The ships had been run aground and left to sink.

Chapter Seven

THE FIELD OF ARROWS

AND TO THINK your uncle wished us to trust our lives to those leaky ships." Mateo crossed himself and rolled his eyes heavenward, but those eyes twinkled and the corners of his mouth twitched. "Who would believe that hungry sea worms could do such terrible damage."

"Sea worms!" Diego sputtered a moment before he could continue. "Two-legged sea worms with brace and bit."

"How can you say that? With my own ears I heard the sailors declare the ships as full of holes as a pauper's cloak. There was nothing to do but run them aground before some foolish soldier sailed away to his death."

"I'd like to know how much of Cortez's gold those sailors carry now."

"Have done," Juan shouted. "How can I work with you squabbling like a pair of carrion crows?"

He was nervous enough without their bickering. His father had set him to dismantling the precious crossbow. Following Mateo's lead, Juan had removed rust from the trigger and pins, then greased the metal parts. Now he must reassemble the weapon and wax the string. His sweaty fingers had trouble setting the trigger spring properly. Already tense under the responsibility, their argument had strained his nerves beyond control.

"The ships are gone. Placing the blame for their loss won't raise them and make them whole." Secretly Juan believed the page was right, that Cortez had contrived the sailors' report and then engineered the town council's decision to declare the ships worthless and sink them. It was the same type of tactics he'd used to manage the demand to found Vera Cruz. The honor of such maneuvers might be questionable, but Juan admired the commander's shrewdness. Not only had he quelled the threatened mutiny, but he'd made certain that the force left behind in Vera Cruz could not desert when he marched to Mexico. For without ships there was no longer any question of returning to Cuba and therefore no reason to delay the meeting with Montezuma.

Juan's blood stirred with excitement. Not only would he see what lay beyond those snow-capped mountains, but he might well have his chance to join the men in battle. Ortega had begun training Juan in the use of the crossbow so that the loss of a bowman would not deprive the army of the weapon itself. Juan refused to think of the danger such preparation implied. It was enough that he was preparing to take his place in the service of God and king.

Already Mateo was stringing his bow. Juan bent to his own work. Ortega had stressed that knowledge of the care and repair of the crossbow was as important as marksmanship. Juan was determined the work would be done properly the first time. In comfortable silence Mateo and Juan assembled and waxed the crossbows while Diego polished his uncle's helmet and cuirass until they shone even in the shade where the three comrades worked. The page glanced furtively around, then drew his own sword and a sharpening stone from beneath the pile of gear. Mateo grinned.

"That's right. Sharpen it well. The pineapples in the mountains will be green and tough."

"I do not plan to fight vegetables," replied the page.

"Look out! Your uncle comes."

Diego thrust the sword under cover and began furiously polishing the already gleaming helmet. Mateo roared with laughter. The page flushed, gathered his uncle's fighting gear, and stalked away. Juan's hands tightened over his father's crossbow. He knew Diego's torment at being with the army but still not of it.

"You shouldn't bait him, Mateo."

"How can I help it? The dumb fish takes the hook so easily."

"Be careful. He may learn the game from you."

"When and if that happens the game is over." He leaned over to inspect the crossbow in Juan's hands. "More wax on the string."

The middle of August they were ready to leave. Almost a thousand Cempoalan warriors joined them and supplied two hundred porters to carry the six small cannons, ammunition, food and baggage. The soldiers carried their weapons and wore the native armor of quilted cotton. It was light, comfortable, and yet deflected the Indian arrows. Mateo's sandals no longer looked strange. Most of the Castilians had worn out their shoes and taken to the native footgear. With Boba ranging off to the sides, Juan stepped eagerly along beside Father Olmedo.

All through the lowlands the villages welcomed and fed them. Then the way of march led up the mountains. The vegetation became sparse and twisted. Cold winds chilled them to the bone. Even the cotton armor was no protection against the sleet and hail. Juan and the priest huddled together during the nights. Father Olmedo stretched the skirt of his robe to cover Juan's shoulders and Boba trembled between them, trading the warmth of her body for some of theirs. Still their teeth chattered and their lips were blue in the cheerless dawn. At last they descended to a warm valley that swore allegiance to Mexico.

The temples ran with fresh blood, and what little food the people provided was given sullenly. Except to Boba. The dog was fed constantly. Juan thought it odd that people who sacrificed humans should have such love of animals, until he overheard one of the porters telling the villagers that the dog was a new kind of lion that devoured Indians if not kept well fed. The horses, they added, were trained to run down enemies and breathed fire on command.

Weapons ready and belts drawn tight against their hunger, the soldiers marched on toward Tlaxcala. The Cempoalans assured Cortez the Tlaxcalans were enemies of Montezuma, always at war with Mexico. Surely they would welcome allies. The Castilians pressed eagerly toward the first village and marched into an ambush. After a brief skirmish the Indians retreated. The village was deserted and bare of food.

The next day's march began with a battle but Juan, staggering in the rear with the baggage train, saw little of the fighting. He had all he could do to place one foot ahead of the other. His head ached and his breath came in short gasps through cracked lips. Someone called his name. He blinked, trying to steady the hazy edges of the figure before him.

"Juan." The voice was Diego's, but the boy that grabbed his arm looked like a dirty urchin from Santiago's plaza. "Juan, what ails you?"

Juan rubbed his forearm over his face. "I must be faint from hunger."

The ragged figure moved aside and a priest's cassock darkened his vision.

"It is the fever," said Father Olmedo.

"Juan! Dear Mother of God, keep your senses for a little while. Juan!"

He pushed away the helping hands and forced himself to focus on the distant words.

"Back to the town," Diego's voice shouted. "Take refuge in the temples. If we must retreat, the pyramids can be defended. Juan, you must tell the porters. Do you understand? Tell the porters."

He nodded, turned, and would have fallen if Father Olmedo had not caught him. He translated the instructions to the nearest porter. After an eternity of stumbling and groping, he found the smooth stone of the pyramid in front of him. With Father Olmedo's help he pulled himself up the high, steep steps. Suddenly priest and boy sank together. Juan had a moment of clear vision. The priest's face was flushed and his eyes feverishly bright. Then the thin, strong hands of the Indian porters were bearing him to the temple at the top.

He woke to the coolness of water. Ortega was bathing his face. Firelight flickered on the temple roof.

"It is over?" The words came thickly through his dry lips.

Ortega nodded. "With God's help we won again."

A tongue licked his hand. Juan rubbed Boba's fur. His hand came away sticky with blood. He struggled to sit up.

"She's hurt."

"Only a few small cuts." Ortega pushed him back on the mat. "She fought at my side today."

Boba had fought. She might have been killed and in his

feverish daze Juan hadn't even missed her. The fever even drowned his pang of guilt.

Ortega forced him to drink broth and water, but Juan wanted only to drift in the half sleep of fever. Dreams woke him often during the night, and each time Boba whined and thumped her tail as if to assure him she was there. In the morning she sat alert, watching the preparations for battle, but when Ortega left she made no move to follow. Juan lay quietly until he was sure his father must be far down the pyramid. Then he crawled out to the wide, open platform.

At first he was conscious only of the beauty. The plains beyond the town were covered with rippling patches of scarlet, white, green and yellow. Then he gasped at the realization that the color was from high feathered head-dresses, tens of thousands of headdresses. The sun glinted on tens of thousands of swords. Below the temple gathered only four hundred Castilians and a thousand Indian allies. What chance had they? Juan fought his dizziness and strained to catch the commander's shouted instructions.

"They have sworn to sacrifice us to their gods, so they will fight more to capture than to kill. Stand shield to shield and don't break ranks no matter what befalls. Thrust for faces or bellies. Bowmen and arquebusiers, fire half and half. With God's help we shall win."

Juan could see his father counting off the bowmen who would fire first and rewind their bows while the second half fired. Lances ready, the horsemen moved forward. The swordsmen marched shield to shield and the bowmen, each protected by a shieldman, moved forward with the arquebusiers. Their Indian allies yelled and trotted forward, black obsidian swords waving.

The mass of feathers rippled excitedly. Trumpets blared, drums sounded and the Indians charged to meet the invaders. Over their screams came Cortez's command, "Santiago and at them!" The Tlaxcalans launched a barrage of arrows so thick it hid the battle from Juan's view. Boba whined and paced nervously. Juan's head dropped against his arms. He prayed, drifted into a fever-ridden doze, then roused to pray again.

He woke cool and dry. The fever had broken. He pushed himself to one elbow and discovered he was back inside the temple. In a patch of sunlight Ortega sorted a pile of arrows. Juan crossed himself with a trembling hand.

"Thank God and St. James. We won."

Ortega smiled at him. "That was two days ago."

"Two days!" Juan groaned. "I missed it again."

"You're not the only one. More men are down with fever than wounds. Father Olmedo can barely stand. Even the commander has it."

"Cortez? Sick?"

"Yes, but it hasn't affected his tongue. He is still trying to win over the Tlaxcalans." He reached behind him for fruit and tortillas. "I saved you this."

As Juan ate he listened to the account of two other attacks, one at night. Each had been followed by attempts to convince the Tlaxcalans that the Castilians wanted only peace.

"I thought the Tlaxcalans were friendly," said Juan.

"If they're friends, then I don't want to make any enemies in this land." Mateo blocked the sunshine as he moved in to Juan's mat. "The fever has left you, I see."

Diego followed on his heels. The page wore a new hat but his doublet and hose were more torn and grimy than Juan remembered from that first day of fever. As they lowered themselves to the stone floor the sun fell across Mateo's face. Juan gasped. The bowman's swollen nose almost hid his eyes, both of which were mottled blue-black. Surely that was no battle wound.

"What happened to you?"

"I broke my nose."

"But how?" Juan glanced at the page. No, it hadn't been Diego.

"The Tlaxcalans fought with slings as well as bows," explained Ortega. "The rocks fell thick as hail. Díaz has a lump on his head the size of your fist and you see Mateo's nose."

"Hardly an honorable wound," sniffed the page.

"I see no lumps or cuts on your head," said Mateo.

Ortega interrupted. "The only thing that saved us was the way they charged, all massed together. Every one of our arrows and shots struck home. Then too we hear the caciques are quarreling among themselves. They attack one at a time instead of joining forces."

"Thank God for that," said Mateo. "You should have seen the plains. The arrows were so thick on the ground it looked like a wheat field ready for harvest."

"A harvest of death," said Diego softly. "Fifty-five of our men are dead. Fifty-five men who would be enjoying their shares this very minute if we had sailed home from Vera Cruz."

Mateo snorted. "That's how little you know of soldiers. The pittance they'd have shared wouldn't have lasted this long in Santiago."

"Your shares are no larger now. We've gathered nothing on this march but wounds, fever, and broken noses."

"Do you see these?" Mateo pulled his worn boots out from his belt. "After I fill these with gold in Mexico you can talk about returning to Cuba and I might listen. Until then you're only fouling good air with your coward's talk of retreat."

Diego jumped to his feet. "I said nothing of retreat and I'm no coward."

"That still remains to be seen."

"Father." Juan's voice was as weak as his gesture, but Ortega understood his plea to intervene.

"There can be no turning back now," he said firmly. "The Tlaxcalans would think they had won. Every tribe, even those now friendly, would attack us. Besides, there are no ships to take us back to Cuba if we did reach the coast."

"Perhaps not yet." The page smiled mysteriously and left.

"Now what deviltry is his uncle plotting," muttered Mateo.

"The ship," said Juan. "The ship Cortez sent to King Charles. Was there a Velásquez man aboard?"

"I don't believe so." Ortega frowned.

"But who can know?" said Mateo.

There was silence as they thought of Governor Velásquez. If the ship stopped at Cuba the governor might keep it from sailing on. Cortez's letters might never reach King Charles. Even if the ship did proceed to Castile, the news of the founding of Vera Cruz would turn the governor purple with anger. Ortega put their fears into words.

"If he comes now to arrest Cortez, we'll be caught between the fire and a hot iron."

Chapter Eight

HOT IRON AND BOILING OIL

THE PYRAMIDS of Tlaxcala were sharply etched against the predawn sky. From one, then another, the temple drums woke the city to another day. Juan tilted his head to hear more clearly over the shuffling of sleepy soldiers. Each morning for two weeks he'd heard the drums and each morning had been sure his ears deceived him. A drum was for marching or savage rituals, not for playing tunes. Yet these drums each had more than one note and played a tune as well as rhythm. It was still savage but with an eerie beauty that Juan appreciated. He patted Boba's head as she settled at the base of the pyramid to await his return.

Mateo puffed as he hoisted himself up the high steps. "By the time I get up there I'm too winded to pray. Couldn't we have had the altar at ground level?"

"Nothing worthwhile is easily reached," Ortega said quietly.

"Then Mexico must be worth six kingdoms."

"Only to those who live to reach it," said another bowman climbing with them.

"We'll reach it." Mateo's voice was harsh with disapproval.

"God willing," added Ortega, crossing himself.

"Then you and Cortez will go by yourselves." The bowman grinned wickedly but they were already inside the temple and the quiet of mass could not be disturbed by argument.

Juan glanced at the kneeling men. How many of them felt the same way? Battle against the Tlaxcalans had done much to win support for the Velásquez faction. If this one rebellious province could call forty thousand warriors to arms, what force was powerful Mexico preparing?

True, the Tlaxcalans had asked for peace, but it had not been a victory of Castilian arms so much as self-defeat of heathen beliefs. Each cacique was guided by the portents of his own priests. They could not agree on a plan of attack or even a time. When a cacique fell in battle the thousands of warriors who followed him deserted. Ridiculous omens caused mass retreat. Thus the handful of Castilians, united and determined, had turned back every attack. When sword arms tired, Cortez rallied them to new strength, hardened them by voice and example to stand firmly against a fresh onslaught and then, when seemingly numb with fatigue, led them to attack and win.

For the first time since the Tlaxcalans had welcomed

them into the city Juan did not give thanks to God and St. James for sparing their lives. He prayed instead for all the powers of heaven to strengthen Cortez this day. The commander once again was facing mutiny, this time openly declared. Everyone knew the Velásquez men were going to demand that Cortez turn back to the coast and build ships. Turn back or be abandoned with those foolhardy enough to remain loyal.

As Father Olmedo's deep voice echoed in the stone temple the horns of the Tlaxcalan priests sounded from the other pyramids. Father Olmedo had refused to let Cortez repeat his action at Cempoala. He held fast to his conviction that the Indians must reject their evil gods themselves. That the Christian God had been willingly given a temple in the midst of paganism was proof the Indians could be won. The women decorated the altar with flowers and many knelt now among the soldiers. Hadn't Doña Marina said it was the women who feared the bloodthirsty gods most? Juan remembered guiltily how even Aunt Maria had fought to keep him from joining the expedition. Despite her rough tongue she cared enough about him to worry. He added a prayer that she might find happiness in her new house on Santiago plaza.

When mass was over Juan rose stiffly, crossed himself, and followed his father into the slanting sunshine. About them spread the city, the central market directly below and rows of shining white houses leading to the fields beyond.

"Now we should explore to the south," said Ortega.

"Today?" How could his father tramp the fields when the fate of the expedition was being decided?

"Especially today. The corn is being harvested."

"And Cortez is receiving Velásquez's men."

"They will argue for hours. Meanwhile tempers will sharpen until harsh words aren't enough. Unless you wish to make enemies it's better to stay away until the captains come to terms."

Juan sighed. "To the fields then."

These last days he'd seen enough corn, beans and squash to permanently dull his appetite, but his father was right. The two factions were ready to fight. Diego and Mateo had been pulling him between them like dogs contesting a bone. If Juan went back to their quarters now he'd lose the friendship of one if not both. This was a time when no one could stand aside, his loyalty undeclared.

Boba rose from her waiting place as they reached the street. Juan held her close until they were through the market. The Indians, terrified by the false stories of this strange "lion," let the dog help herself at their stalls. Juan had discovered that Tlaxcala, for all its size, was a poor city. Constant wars with Mexico drained it of men and supplies. Districts under Mexican taxation refused to trade with the rebellious province. The Tlaxcalans had only what they could produce themselves.

Once out of the city he let the greyhound run free. Most of

the morning they roamed the neat square fields. Juan translated his father's questions with only half his mind. The other part worried over what was being decided back in the city.

If Cortez failed to win over the Velásquez men, would the commander return to Cuba or march alone to Mexico? And if the army divided, which way would Ortega go? Juan looked often toward the smoking volcano that marked the way to Montezuma's city. He would like to see what lay beyond but not if it meant ending on one of the bloody altars. He shuddered.

Ortega looked at him anxiously. "Fever again?"

"No." He looked at the sun. "Do you think it's decided now?"

Ortega snorted. "It was decided in Santiago. Cortez has selected his own destiny. Only death will keep him from reaching Mexico."

"But Diego's uncle and the rest."

"Fools, all of them, to throw away everything when we are so close. What have we to gain by returning? We will only have suffered these past months for nothing." He too looked at the volcano. "I wonder if Ordaz and his men reached the top."

The soldier Ordaz had asked permission to climb the smoking mountain. Cortez had consented when he learned the Tlaxcalans considered it impossible. If the Castilians succeeded in spite of the gods said to dwell in the mountains, the Indians would hold them in even greater awe. Juan grinned. Diego was right in calling Cortez a lawyer. The commander never passed up an opportunity to strengthen his case. Juan hoped he could defeat the argument being presented to him today.

They returned to the city to find their quarters in an uproar.

"We returned too soon," said Juan.

"Ortega," called Díaz. "Come give us your opinion."

"You already have it. I'm for Mexico."

The group of men turned to stare at him. Díaz laughed. "We all are, old friend. We have all offered our souls to God and dedicated our bodies and swords to the service of the king. We follow Cortez to Mexico."

"Then why are these fools gabbling?"

"The Tlaxcalans have advised us to take a longer route to avoid Cholula. They say the Cholulans are not to be trusted."

Ortega snorted. "The Cempoalans said the Tlaxcalans were friends and look what happened. I say the shortest route."

Díaz nodded. "I agree."

A swordsman protested and Díaz tried to shout him down. Juan wandered among the groups of soldiers. Some said Montezuma had sent a hundred thousand men to Cholula to ambush the Castilians. Others said the Cholulans themselves were preparing traps. The arguments were interrupted by the arrival of ambassadors from Mexico with presents of more than two thousand pesos' worth of gold. Montezuma would send that much and more to the coast each year if Cortez would not come to Mexico. The admission of fear swept away all doubts. The army united in their determination to march, and by the shortest route. The Cempoalans agreed to continue with them, and the Tlaxcalans added two thousand warriors.

The next day Ordaz returned from scaling the volcano. From its summit he and his men had seen Mexico, an enormous city gleaming in the center of a lake. Three other great cities sprawled on the lake shores. Mateo's eyes glittered as he patted his nearly empty boots, but Ortega turned away and crossed himself. A chill settled over Juan's heart.

He remembered One-Eye's prediction that they'd find only enough land to cover their bodies. He fingered the knife he'd kept hidden, then tore open his doublet. Defiantly he fastened the knife sheath to his belt. His father glanced at the weapon but said nothing. Each time Juan touched it for reassurance Boba tensed as if he'd signaled danger. Juan smoothed her bristled neck hair.

"There's nothing, girl," he murmured soothingly.

The closer they came to Cholula the more the dog worried him. She stopped her private explorations of the countryside and kept pace with Juan and Father Olmedo, her ears and nose testing the air. The priest must have noticed also, for when the Cholulans came to meet them, singing and burning copal incense, he laughed.

"Your dog is truly named, Juanito. Or perhaps all those prayers her nervousness inspired have been heard."

The Cempoalans and Tlaxcalans camped outside the city, but the Castilians were given spacious rooms opening from a large courtyard. For two days they were well treated, though men returning from the market brought news of streets mysteriously walled off. Díaz sought out Ortega and suggested a stroll. Juan rose and called Boba.

"Stay here," his father ordered.

"Let him come," said Díaz. "It will look better with the boy along. Besides, he understands their tongue. He may hear something that will help."

Juan glanced from one to the other. "Then the Tlaxcalans were right."

The soldier shrugged. "Only God knows. Cortez has heard that Montezuma's ambassadors have arrived but not to see us, though we plan to march tomorrow."

As they passed through the courtyard gate Juan's father warned him, "Keep your ears open but say nothing of what you hear until we return."

Juan was so engrossed in eavesdropping while pretending deafness that he forgot about Boba until he heard angry shouts and a yelp of pain.

"That was Boba." He spun round, searching the crowd.

"There." Ortega pointed to a cluster of silent Indians.

They pushed their way through to find Boba hunched on the ground, her tail between her legs. A merchant threatened her with a stick. Between them lay a leopard skin. The paw near Boba was mangled from her chewing. Juan seized the greyhound's collar and pulled her back.

"That foreign beast should be made into stew," shouted the merchant.

"You'll have its skin to replace the leopard," said one of the bystanders.

Ortega hissed a warning at Juan. They let Díaz ask by signs if the merchant would accept a small gold lizard for the leopard skin. When the trade had been made the merchant touched the ground three times respectfully and spoke calmly. Juan stiffened and glanced at the ring of impassive Indian faces.

"Let's get back to quarters." He hauled the protesting Boba away. Now that they had bought the mangled leopard skin she'd switched her interest to a small black pelt.

When they were inside the courtyard gate Juan turned to the two men. "That merchant wasn't thanking you, Díaz. He wished we three might be among the twenty they've promised to their gods."

There was silence. Then Díaz asked, "Did he say when?"

"No, but Doña Marina said one of their bloody festivals is to be held the day after tomorrow."

"I must see the commander."

Juan could watch the news spreading as one group of men

left their gambling and the laughter of another died. Weapons were inspected for flaws that didn't exist. Men paced restlessly to the courtyard and back. After dark two Cempoalans brought news that all women and children were leaving Cholula. Tlaxcalan sentries had discovered twenty thousand Mexican soldiers hidden in ravines outside the city. No one needed to be told that the two thousand Cholulans who had offered to accompany the Castilians in the morning would be part of the ambush.

"We are not sheep who wait quietly to be slaughtered," said Cortez. He issued orders and well before dawn all was ready.

Cortez sat calmly on his horse. Soldiers lounged around him with their packs ready to march. The treacherous Cholulans who planned to escort them into ambush crowded eagerly into the courtyard. Cortez signaled. Swordsmen raised their shields and stood shoulder to shoulder across the courtyard gate. Bowmen and arquebusiers appeared at windows and doors, weapons loaded and aimed. Juan was forced back from his vantage point, but he could hear.

A hush fell over the crowded court. Then Cortez spoke. Doña Marina stepped out to translate his accusation of treason. Treason, he explained, could not go unpunished. He raised his hand. An arquebusier touched match to his gun and fired. Juan held the struggling Boba as he watched his father load and fire the crossbow. Shouts, screams, and the clash of swords rose to frantic pitch. Then bowmen and arquebusiers raced for the doors. The noise of battle faded. Boba stood quietly, only her ears moving as she followed the sound of distant battle.

Diego dropped to the floor beside Juan. They waited in silence, each wrapped in his own fears and prayers. They half rose when sounds of fighting reached them, then slumped back against the wall as the cries faded. From time to time bare feet ran past the building, but four hours passed before the Castilians trudged into the courtyard. Ortega returned carrying his bow in his left hand, his right arm bloody from a gash that laid open the bone from shoulder to elbow. Following his father's instructions, Juan cauterized the wound with a hot iron and boiling oil, then ran to the courtyard and was sick. When he returned Diego was tying the bandage. The page grinned crookedly.

"The first wound I treated went without a bandage too."

Juan waved at the heating irons and oil. "You've done this before?"

"When you were raving with fever." The page rose. "Unfortunately Mateo hasn't even a broken nose this time. I'd enjoy treating a wound for him. Come, there are others who need our aid."

Juan helped though his stomach lurched at the smell of seared flesh. The wounds were many but there were no deaths. The Cempoalans and Tlaxcalans had joined the battle once the fighting broke out of the court and into the city. Montezuma's warriors had taken no part. They disappeared from the ravines as quietly as they had come.

Ambassadors continued to bring excuses from Mexico. Though they brought gold, they declared the city was poor. The Castilians would starve if they went to Mexico. Montezuma was ill and would be unable to see Cortez. Finally they swore that a horde of lions, jaguars, and other beasts would devour the Castilians should they enter the city. And all the time the Mexicans protested, the Castilians and their Indian allies marched steadily toward the shining city in the lake.

Chapter Nine

MONTEZUMA

"IT'S LIKE A DREAM." Juan ran his hand lightly over the cotton-covered walls and fingered the tasseled canopy over his sleeping mat. He paused by the door and breathed deeply of the flower-scented air. Boba barked down by the stone-edged pond. Juan decided against calling her in. It wouldn't hurt the ducks to be chased one night. Tomorrow they were entering Mexico.

He had seen it today at the other end of the causeway, gleaming silver against the blue lake. If this lake-edge city where they spent the night left him dazed, what was Mexico like? This city had over twelve thousand houses. How many were on that island in the center of the lake? He searched his memory to compare sizes, but he'd been so excited he couldn't be sure what he had seen.

"Juan, you're next."

He took his place on the stool to have his hair trimmed. Those who had fine clothes dug them from the baggage. Others washed and brushed their old ones. Everything that could be polished was scoured and buffed. Juan's preparations didn't take long, but he knew Diego must be working far into the night. He lay on the mat a long time before Boba stretched out against him with a contented sigh. Juan rubbed her wet fur absently.

"November eighth," he whispered. "That's a day to remember, Boba. The day we meet the emperor of Mexico."

Juan had seen many parades in Castile, but not even the grandest had held the tense excitement of the procession on the causeway next morning. The advance guard of four mounted soldiers crisscrossed the causeway as they advanced. Their armor glittered and the bells on the horses' breastplates tinkled. Boba trotted behind them, sniffing the strange Indians on one side and then the other. Diego followed slowly, carrying the yellow-and-scarlet standard of Castile. Juan's throat tightened as he watched the banner circle and dip in the ceremonial patterns. Next marched the swordsmen, shields in one hand and bared blades in the other. After them clattered half the cavalry. Then came the bowmen. Juan stepped out proudly between his father and Mateo. Though he had no plumed helmet, he wore cotton armor and slung his father's crossbow over his right shoulder. Ortega carried the quiver under his uninjured arm. Behind them thudded more horsemen, then the arquebusiers. Finally, in full glittering armor, rode Cortez surrounded by standard bearers. Behind danced the Indian allies in feathered mantles and high colorful plumes.

The soldiers marveled at the paved causeways, wondering how the Indians had managed to span the lake with these man-made strips of land wide enough for eight horsemen to ride abreast. The road across the lake was so crowded with people the soldiers could hardly pass for fear of crowding some of the staring on-lookers into the lake. They were forced to halt at a towered fortress built where a smaller causeway joined the one on which they marched. Nearly a thousand Mexicans in bright-feathered cloaks came to touch their fingers to the ground, then to their lips in sign of homage to Cortez. At last the marchers passed through the fort. Here the causeway had been built wide enough to squeeze a row of brightly painted houses along one edge. The roofs were as crowded as the strip of road.

Every once in a while Ortega grunted. When the crowd forced the marchers together he spoke across Juan to Mateo, "Have you noticed the bridges?"

"Bridges?"

"Stop weighing the value of their ornaments and take notice of things that matter. These causeways aren't solid. Every so often there is a bridge opening to let the water through and keep the lake from becoming foul and stagnant."

"The openings let their boats pass through also," Juan added.

His father nodded. "But there are other uses for the bridges."

They tramped over another bridge and Mateo said, "You are right, Ortega. Pull out a few beams and the bridges can be easily lifted. The city is as safe as a Castilian fortress."

"Unless you are inside and wish to leave," Ortega warned.

The young bowman grinned at a group of Indian girls. "Who wishes to leave? I'm going to like it here."

"Fool."

At the end of the causeway they wheeled smartly and stood at attention. People crowded the streets and the terraced roofs of large houses. From the corner of his eyes Juan watched two lines of caciques approach. They wore their finest cloaks and jewels, but their feet were bare. Four more caciques came, sweeping the ground and laying mats where Montezuma might walk. Behind them bobbed a green-feathered canopy bordered with gold, silver and pearls. Beneath, in a litter, rode a man about Ortega's age. His black hair hung to his waist, but his beard was small and sparse. He moved smoothly, lean and muscular as a practiced swordsman. When Montezuma stepped out onto the mats Juan heard Mateo moan softly. The soles of the emperor's sandals were made of gold.

Cortez dismounted and strode forward. When he tried to embrace the emperor, the caciques held his arms. No one touched the emperor and only the Castilians looked directly at Montezuma. The Indians kept their eyes on the ground in his presence.

116

Montezuma touched the ground and kissed the earth on his fingers.

"Welcome, our lord. You have come at last to your people, to your home. You have come to claim the chair and the mat which I have guarded for you. Others have cared for it before me. Would that one of them were alive now and this had happened in his time. But they are dead. They said you would return to sit on your chair and rule these lands. Now I see that what they said is true. You are here. Welcome."

Cortez bowed his head to receive Montezuma's gift of two red shell necklaces, each hung with eight gold shrimp. Through Doña Marina he replied.

"You have nothing to fear. You will be harmed by no one. Not by me nor any who come with me. We have long wished to meet and know you. Now at last our wish is fulfilled."

He stepped forward and placed a necklace of colored beads strung on gold cord around Montezuma's neck. Then the caciques who had come with the emperor stepped forward to kiss the earth before Cortez. When the ceremony was finished Montezuma led the way through the city to the great plaza, then into the palace that had belonged to his father. In the courtyard he motioned Cortez to a seat decorated with gold and jewels.

"This is your house. Eat, rest and enjoy yourself. I shall return soon."

Cortez bowed. The emperor and the caciques left. The soldiers relaxed with audible sighs.

An army of servants had already prepared a meal. Juan, his father, and Mateo ate before beginning a tour of inspection. They were soon lost in the maze of gardens, courtyards and passages. The palace was not one building but a fortress of several joined by wide walls. Some of the rooms could easily house a hundred and fifty soldiers. Mateo whistled softly.

"No one in Castile will ever believe it."

Ortega raised his hand. "Listen."

They traced the thuds and curses, to find soldiers mounting the cannon on the roof and walls. Mateo snorted.

"Next thing he'll be assigning guard duty."

"He already has," said a passing soldier. "And orders are not to leave this palace."

"That's no hardship. Even with a couple of thousand Indians in here with us we have room to get lost."

For four days they were restricted to the palace. While his father's arm healed Juan shouldered the crossbow and stood his turn at sentry duty. Father Olmedo was always waiting for him to translate to the servants Montezuma had provided. It left him little time to explore, and Boba wasn't the only one restless for the freedom of the city.

On the fourth day Father Olmedo brought a soldier to the wall to relieve Juan.

"Cortez is sending Doña Marina and Aguilar to see

Montezuma," explained the priest. "I've asked that you go with them."

Juan didn't ask why he'd been included for fear Father Olmedo might reconsider. He hastily brushed his clothes and borrowed hose and a cap from Diego. Doña Marina stared at the unaccustomed finery.

"Do you wear such fine clothes when you go before your own emperor?" she asked.

"Of course. We must honor him by wearing our best, poor though it may be."

"How strange that is. We must put on the poorest of cloaks and go barefoot into Montezuma's presence to show our humility."

"A Castilian humbles himself only to God." Juan added hastily, "But that is not why I wear borrowed finery. This is to do honor to Montezuma as I would to my own emperor."

Juan wished he could follow the Indian custom. His legs felt encased in armor and the sugarloaf hat kept sliding over his ear. But he soon forgot his discomfort.

Montezuma's palace was even larger than the one in which they were quartered. Twenty gates opened from the four walls that enclosed huge gardens and a hundred large rooms. The wood-framed walls were filled with marble, jasper, and a black stone with red veins that Juan thought better suited to the temples. They were led from one room to another, past walls covered with feathered cloth and others with rabbit hair. Juan gaped at the cedar ceilings carved with grotesque birds and animals. Doña Marina touched his arm and he saw they were in the presence of Montezuma.

A cacique in a plain coarse cloak backed toward the door, his eyes on his bare feet. When he was gone Juan followed Aguilar and Doña Marina across the room. The Indian woman walked stiffly as if concentrating all her strength on keeping her eyes level with the emperor's. Habit was too strong. When she spoke her eyes lowered to the floor as custom demanded.

Montezuma greeted them warmly but his eyes were alert and wary. When Doña Marina delivered Cortez's message that he wished to visit their great temple, the dark eyes brightened and he smiled. Juan shifted uneasily as he listened.

During the past days Cortez had made several visits to explain the true faith to Montezuma, with little success. It was obvious from Montezuma's reply that he thought Cortez was courteously requesting a similar explanation of the Mexican religion. Such a misunderstanding might lead to trouble at the temple. Juan was still debating whether or not to disillusion the emperor, when Doña Marina bowed three times and turned to the door. The interview was over. It was too late to do anything except warn Father Olmedo. As he walked back with Aguilar, Juan realized this was exactly the reason he'd been sent.

There were dozens of pyramids in the city. One large one

rose opposite their quarters, but Cortez had chosen to visit the largest, the only one topped by two temples. Caciques were sent to guide them across the city. Juan was glad he'd left Boba tied in the palace, for the way led through the market. Like everything else in Mexico it was so vast and complex it made him dizzy.

All the products of every province under Mexican domination were sold or bartered here. There were gems and precious metals, everything in weaving from the sisal thread to the finished feather-embroidered cloth, rope, shoes, furs and leather, vegetables and cocoa, animals and birds both live and dressed, pottery, mats and honey cakes, firewood, salt, tobacco-filled pipes, herbs, ointments, obsidian knives, and gold in goosequill containers. There were not just one or two stalls of each kind but entire streets devoted to one product. Over it all sat three judges to settle disputes and punish thieves.

They passed from the market through an arch and into a huge square. In the center rose the Great Pyramid, three hundred and fifty feet square. As they crossed the spotless white paving Montezuma appeared at the top of the pyramid. Six priests hurried down to support Cortez and his captains under the arms as they climbed. Cortez waved them away and began climbing at a pace that had most of the soldiers puffing. Juan counted the steep narrow steps.

"A hundred and fourteen," he informed Father Olmedo.

"Is that all?" the priest managed between heaving breaths. Montezuma stepped forward to greet Cortez. "I am sure you are tired after climbing this great temple of ours."

"Not at all," lied the commander. "Neither I nor any of these with me ever tire."

Juan followed reluctantly into the temple. The sacrificial stone outside was wet with fresh blood. He dreaded what he might see inside. He stood close to Father Olmedo, answering his questions when Aguilar's brusque translation failed to satisfy the priest's curiosity.

In the first hall were four giant idols. The one circled by golden snakes and holding bow and arrows was the god of war. Three hearts burned in the brazier before it. Opposite was their god of the world-after-death, mirror eyes gleaming in a bear's face. Five hearts burned before it.

"Sacrifices to the gods of war and hell," murmured Father Olmedo. "I wonder if it has special meaning for us."

"I don't believe so. Doña Marina says there are special sacrifices and ceremonies for almost every day of the year."

"May God have mercy on the souls of the victims." He pointed to a statue half man and half dragon. "What is that creature?"

Juan caught only the end of Aguilar's translation. "It must be their farm god. Its body is supposed to contain all the seeds in the world."

He wished Cortez would hurry. The place stank worse than a slaughterhouse, and the Indian priests were sickening with their blood-matted hair and ears tattered from personal sacrifices of blood.

Cortez began to speak. "Lord Montezuma, how can such a wise man as yourself fail to see these idols are not gods but devils? I can show you and your priests how evil they are. Let me put a cross on top of this temple and set an image of Our Lady in here. Then you'll see how your idols tremble in fear."

As Aguilar translated, Montezuma's face hardened.

"If I had thought you would insult our gods I would never have shown them to you," said the emperor. "They are not evil but good. They have given us health, harvests, and victory over our enemies. I warn you, do not dishonor them again."

Father Olmedo moved forward to stand beside Cortez.

"Patience," he said softly. "When a sick man needs a purgative the physician gives it in doses the patient can easily swallow. If he pours it down all at once he may lose the patient altogether."

Cortez nodded and said, "It is time for us to go."

"I must stay and atone for the evil you have done," said Montezuma.

"If that is true, forgive me." Cortez bowed and turned away.

When they stepped out on the wide platform Juan gulped air like a freshly caught fish. Cortez fingered his sword hilt as he gazed over the city and lake. They could see all three causeways, one to Guadalupe opposite the one on which they'd entered Mexico and between them one only half as long leading to Tecuba. Canoes darted back and forth, following canals that led all the way to the market and Great Pyramid. The market place alone was larger than the whole city of Tlaxcala.

"I've been all over Italy and as far as Constantinople," said a soldier, "and never have I seen anything like this."

"Never have I seen a city so clean," said Father Olmedo. "There is no litter or filth in any of the streets."

Cortez remained silent, his eyes darting from one causeway to the other. They gleamed in the sun like three silver ropes binding the city to the shore. The Mexicans had only to remove the bridges to break those slender ropes, withhold the supply of food, or besiege the palace where they stayed and the Castilians would be at their mercy.

Juan hoped Cortez would continue to listen to the priest's counsel of patience. Montezuma's words had been clear warning of what would happen if the commander toppled idols down these steps.

The next afternoon Juan and Mateo were fishing in a garden pond when Father Olmedo again asked Juan to accompany the two interpreters to Montezuma's palace.

"I hate to tie Boba again," Juan said. The dog was digging happily around the roots of a flowering shrub. She was not yet allowed outside the palace, and she tried to sneak out as soon as no one watched her.

"I'll see she doesn't leave this garden," said Mateo.

"The palace is just across the square. I won't be gone long."

Though Montezuma kept them waiting more than an hour, he received them courteously. His mouth tightened when Doña Marina mentioned his refusal to let Cortez place an altar in the Great Pyramid. Juan was sure he would refuse permission to build a chapel in the palace where the Castilians were quartered, but Montezuma said the stone masons would be sent tomorrow. Then he smiled.

"Have you nothing to ask for yourselves?"

"No, my lord," murmured Doña Marina.

Aguilar seemed too stunned to answer. Juan lowered his eyes and shook his head. Five minutes later he regretted not asking forgiveness in advance for any damage Boba might do. Apparently the greyhound had trailed Juan as far as the room where they'd waited, but when Juan spied the dog, her ears were cocked forward as she trotted purposefully in the opposite direction from her master.

"You go on," Juan told the others. "I'll catch her."

The halls and rooms were thronged with nobles and servants. Juan held himself to a fast walk. By the time he'd traced Boba through two carved doorways she'd disappeared into a garden. He walked softly around a fountain, peering into the shrubbery and flowers. Squawking ducks gave her away. Juan ran over the twisting paths to the far side of the garden. Boba sniffed along the edge of a pond filled with ducks, cranes, and long-legged pink birds. She ignored the birds until she'd worked into striking distance. Then she dove into their midst, scattering them in panic with her splashing and snapping.

"Boba!"

She glanced at Juan, shook herself dry, and bounded away. The chase led through a series of large buildings. Juan forgot Boba as he gaped at the collection of parrots and strange birds, lions, jaguars, wolves, and small doglike creatures pacing restlessly back and forth in their prisons. He discovered one of the long-nosed animals he'd tried to tame at Vera Cruz. It leaned against the side of the cage and let him scratch its back. Clay jars high as his shoulder held snakes and lizards on feather nests. Juan gaped unbelievingly at a pair of snakes with rattles on their tails. He had just decided they were poisonous vipers when Boba growled.

All through the buildings she'd been barking, yapping, and worrying the animals, but this growl was unlike any sound Juan had ever heard her make. It rumbled from deep in her chest turning to a snarl in her throat. His touch silenced her, but he felt the angry growl still vibrating beneath his hand. Footsteps crunched on the path outside the animal building. Juan pressed flat against the wall, edged toward the door, and peered out.

Cloaks and ornaments identified the three Indians on the path as members of the hill tribes near Cempoala. Then Juan recognized one, a cacique who had come twice to Vera

Cruz. Boba stood rigid against his legs, her eyes on the bloody bundle one carried. Black hair curled from the edges of the covering mats. Juan guessed they were bringing another small animal for Montezuma's collection. Then the Indian paused to resettle his burden. The mats parted and Juan stared in horror at a black curly Castilian beard.

Chapter Ten

THE GODS SPEAK

I swear by the Holy Mother I never meant to let her get out."

Juan shouldered past Mateo but the bowman followed, babbling his apologies and explanations.

"It went completely out of my head. If you'd been here you'd understand. When I heard about the treasure room and then saw . . . Juanito! Surely you're not going to bother the commander with a little thing like letting a dog loose. After all, you brought her back."

Juan left Mateo standing helplessly outside the building where Cortez and the captains were quartered. The sentry grinned at the dog but directed him to Cortez without any questions.

The commander listened quietly, but the veins in his temple swelled and throbbed as his anger built.

"You are sure it was a head?"

Juan nodded. Cortez paced back and forth, then turned and looked sternly at Juan.

128

"I think it's best if you say nothing of this to anyone until we hear what has happened at Vera Cruz. Some men are quick to imagine the worst."

Juan knew which soldiers he meant. He gave his promise willingly, but it was almost more than he could bear to hold back his dreadful secret in the midst of the jubilant company of bowmen. Even Ortega's eyes glistened as he tried to describe the enormous room filled with gold and jewels.

"It's so huge that some of the storage chests are large enough for the two of us to live in comfortably," he exclaimed.

"I think I shall fill one boot with gold and one with jewels," dreamed Mateo.

While debating the best place to build the chapel, the carpenters had noticed a portion of wall that looked newer than the rest. They'd broken through, to find the room where Montezuma's father had stored the collection of a lifetime. Each soldier was permitted to enter and look before the wall was resealed. Only Juan had missed it. When he told of his own discoveries they laughed.

"Snakes with rattles? You've been looking at too many idols."

He bit his lip, wishing he could tell of the last thing he'd seen in Montezuma's garden.

Late that night two Tlaxcalans brought the news Cortez dreaded. Allies of Mexico had attacked the garrison at Vera Cruz, killing seven men and a horse. The entire coast threatened revolt against the Castilians. There was no doubt that Montezuma's ambassadors were behind it.

Juan was pacing out morning sentry duty on the palace roof when Castilian soldiers moved in double time across the plaza, separating to block off all the streets and arches. Then Cortez, five captains, and thirty fully armed soldiers marched across the square to Montezuma's palace. Two hours later they returned accompanied by the emperor himself. The nobles and servants who followed wept openly. Cortez might call Montezuma an honored guest, but all Mexico knew he was a prisoner.

The contented hum of the city changed pitch and rose ominously. The soldiers slept with their weapons, not even easing their rest by removing sandals or cotton armor. Four times the Mexicans began digging through the palace walls to free Montezuma. Once the emperor tried to leap from a roof to his people waiting fifty feet below but the sentries caught him. Then Cortez granted Montezuma's request to visit the Grand Pyramid on condition the emperor accept the "protection" of a hundred and fifty soldiers and make no human sacrifice. Montezuma agreed but the soldiers discovered four young men had been sacrificed the night before in preparation for the emperor's visit. After consulting for hours with the priests, Montezuma returned strangely quiet.

He summoned the caciques responsible for the attack on Vera Cruz and turned them over to Cortez, who promptly put them to death in the plaza. Messengers from the coast reported all was now well at Vera Cruz. Montezuma made no more attempts to escape. The city relaxed, though no one could say if the people had resigned themselves to the situation or were only soothing Castilian fears while they plotted in secret.

Since they'd been in Mexico Juan had seen little of Diego. Not only was the page kept busy, but the division between soldiers and captains, swordsmen and bowmen, had become sharply defined when quarters were assigned in the palace. Two days after the execution Mateo interrupted the noon meal to growl, "Here comes that overdressed popinjay to sour my stomach."

The page strutted through the roomful of staring bowmen, looking like one of Montezuma's brightly plumaged birds in a covey of sparrows. What finery he wasn't wearing he carried heaped in his arms.

"The laundry is that way." Mateo pointed toward the garden. "Or did your uncle come to his senses and throw you out?"

The page ignored him. He dropped the clothes beside Juan. "Some of these should fit well enough."

"Many thanks but I'm comfortable as I am." Juan eyed the long hose and wrinkled but still stiff neck ruffs with distaste. The only change of clothing he wanted was the permanent ownership of cotton armor and plumed bowman's helmet.

"Montezuma has asked for you."

"Then a clean doublet will be enough."

"You don't understand. The emperor wants you to serve him."

Men nearby turned to stare. Juan looked to his father.

"This is an army of Castile," Ortega reminded him. "You may refuse if you wish."

"I just don't want to be a spy."

"It was Montezuma's request," said Diego sharply.

That meant nothing. Cortez was expert at maneuvering others into making requests for him. Then again, it was only natural that Montezuma would want someone near who understood both tongues. Aguilar tended to brooding surliness and Doña Marina was devoted to Cortez. The emperor had no choice. Juan grinned. He was in a position to make a few demands himself.

"I'll do it but only if I may wear my own clothes."

Diego scooped up his rejected treasures and left. He returned to announce testily that no one seemed concerned with the dignity of the page's office. Juan could wear what he wished.

For days Juan puzzled over the reason for his presence in the royal household. Hundreds of servants and relatives served the emperor's every need, obeying orders almost before they were given. So far as Juan could discover, his main duty was to sit cross-legged on a mat in the corner of Montezuma's council room while the emperor received the relatives and caciques through whom he continued to rule his kingdom. Reports from the temples mixed with complaints of unswept roads, reports of tax collections, and plans to repair the fresh water system. After hours of patiently listening to complaints and petitions, Montezuma bathed, changed his clothing, and drank chocolate. Juan was free until late in the day when Cortez and his captains came to amuse the emperor with stories and games.

Always Cortez made a speech explaining the Holy Faith which Juan carefully translated. Montezuma listened courteously but continued to visit the Great Pyramid whenever permitted. After the Castilians left, Montezuma would always ask Juan if there was anything he wished or needed before dismissing him. After a supper chosen from more than thirty separate dishes, the emperor called in jugglers, magicians, or dancers to entertain him. He seemed content save when his glance fell upon the sentries pacing before the doors, a reminder he was a prisoner in his father's palace.

Juan was not long in discovering that Montezuma rose frequently at night to stand in the gardens and study the stars. He was always there before dawn, thrusting agave thorns through his arms, legs, or ear lobes, then sprinkling the drops of blood toward the sky. Only after the sun rose did he return to his chambers, bathe, dress, and breakfast on hot peppers. Juan watched the ritual several mornings on his way to prayers before he found courage to question Montezuma about it.

He chose an afternoon when Cortez had left early and

Montezuma had ordered chocolate for himself and his page. Fearing he might anger the emperor but burning with curiosity, Juan mentioned what he had seen in the garden before dawn.

"Is it one of the lord Montezuma's duties?" he finished.

"It is the duty of all who serve Uitzilopochtli," explained Montezuma. "The god Uitzilopochtli is a young warrior. He dies each night and is reborn every morning. But to be reborn he must fight with his brothers, the stars, and his sister, the moon. Each dawn that he puts them to flight wins another day of life for men. Thus each morning Uitzilopochtli must be fed so that he remains young and strong, for the battle is great and the stars he fights are countless."

Juan tried not to grimace. "And you feed him your blood?"

"Mine is but a small offering. Uitzilopochtli requires much more."

So young men were marched to the sacrificial altars. Juan's feelings must have shown, for Montezuma added, "How could gods eat the coarse food of men? Only the precious liquid of life can nourish them. But in return, the gods assure continued life for men."

Out of respect for the emperor Juan didn't argue. When he reported this heathen belief to Father Olmedo, the priest nodded slowly.

"It shows the truth of what I've feared. There is no way we can forcefully separate Mexico from her false gods without destroying both, not while Montezuma rules. And from what you have told me of the morning councils, I doubt if we could govern this great kingdom without him."

Suddenly Juan realized why Montezuma had requested his services. So that he would carry such information to Father Olmedo and thus to Cortez. It was the same as spying and Juan angrily resented being used in such fashion. But next morning when he knelt at prayers, asking blessings and guidance through the coming day, Juan thought of Montezuma staring at the eastern sky, rigid with fear that the sun might never rise. And Juan felt only pity for the emperor and his people.

Juan was not surprised when Cortez began pressing Montezuma to swear allegiance to King Charles. Until this was done Cortez could not legally claim conquest. Montezuma made several pilgrimages to the temple of his gods, returning with head bowed. At last he called together the rulers of his great cities and provinces. Juan, seated in the background, heard repeated the legend of Quetzalcoatl, this time in detail. As Montezuma repeated the prophecy to his caciques Juan realized why the powerful Mexicans had wavered between war and peace.

The white-robed Quetzalcoatl had been fair-skinned with a heavy beard. He had preached against the offering of blood. Sickened by the continued sacrifice of humans, he had gone to the coast and sailed into the rising sun. Before he left he declared he would return in the year of One Reed.

His religion would then be accepted and his sons and brothers would rule Mexico.

"This is the year of One Reed," said Montezuma. "These fair men come from the land of the sun. You have heard what they said in the Great Temple and what they did at Cempoala. I believe these are the ones we were told would come."

"But they are not gods," said a cacique. "They bleed and they die."

"No one without the strength of gods could fight as they do."

There were murmurs of assent.

"That is not all. Again and again I have sacrificed to the great god Uitzilopochtli. The first time he said, 'I have given you an answer. Do not ask me again.' Since then he does not speak."

"There is no sign?"

"The gods are silent."

Shortly before Christmas, in the presence of the royal notary, Montezuma and his caciques swore allegiance to King Charles. Juan watched the ceremony through a blur of tears. When he blinked them away he saw many men weeping. Not even Cortez was dry-eyed. There is no joy in the conquest of an enemy one respects.

During the winter Mexico became home to the Castilians. Montezuma continued to rule the Indians and visit the Great Pyramid but only with Cortez's approval. The soldiers kept busy hunting, trading, exploring the surrounding country, and settling disputes in the provinces.

Juan spent most of his time with Montezuma. His role was not that of servant but companion. The emperor questioned him about Castile, Cuba, and the customs of his people. He thought it strange Juan should have a dog as companion. Dogs were bred for food in Mexico, but he let Juan bring Boba from the bowmen's quarters. Her comforting presence more than made up for the added problem of curbing her indiscriminate gnawing.

From their hours of conversation Juan learned much about the Mexicans. He was bewildered by their detailed system of records, their calendar, and the free mixture of legend with their history. He was awed by their government and arts, and though he detested their bloody religion, he could not help admiring Montezuma's fervid devotion.

"What a priest he would have made," mourned Father Olmedo during one of their frequent meetings.

"He *is* a priest," said Juan. "He's head priest to their greatest god. That's why Cortez might as well save his breath. Montezuma is one Mexican who will never be converted."

"The commander is too impatient." The priest warmed his hands over a glowing brazier. "The greatest things in life—freedom, faith, even knowledge—cannot be forced on people. They will be shed just as a bit of wet paper drops from a wall when it dries."

"But how can they learn the true faith unless they are taught?"

"Teaching is not force. It is guidance. We can guide them to faith and knowledge, but the desire for it must come from within themselves. Need and desire are the glues that make faith stick." He sighed. "God knows they have the need."

Near the end of winter the wall Mateo patted fondly whenever he passed was broken open, and Juan at last saw the fabulous jewel room. Besides statues and ornaments made of gold and silver there were swords and blowguns set with jewels, feather pictures of jeweled birds, gold plates, and elaborate headdresses. The gold alone made three piles, each worth more than six hundred thousand pesos. Juan couldn't bear to watch when the intricately worked bracelets, necklaces, and statues were melted into bars.

With the division of the gold, arguments began. Diego's uncle crossed swords with another captain and spent a night in chains. Brawls were common and Mateo's nose was broken again. When Father Olmedo appeared at Montezuma's door, white-faced and shaken, Juan's first thought was of his father.

"Ortega is as safe as any of us." The priest drew him to a secluded corner. "What is that god Montezuma serves?"

"Uitzilopochtli."

"That's the one. Cortez went to the Great Pyramid today and smashed that idol with an iron bar."

"No!"

The priest sighed. "I wish that were all. He's sent for a cross and a statue of Our Lady. He's putting them in the temple."

"This is the end of peace," Juan said. And it couldn't have happened at a worse time. All but a handful of the soldiers were outside the city. It would take a week to recall them.

"You have answered my question before it was asked," said Father Olmedo. "You believe Montezuma will order an attack."

"I know he will."

Days passed uneventfully and it seemed Juan had been wrong. Then some priests and nobles came to confer with Montezuma. The emperor took them to an inner room. They were still talking when Juan woke the next morning. Near midday they left, and Montezuma asked Juan to summon Cortez.

"Tell him Uitzilopochtli has spoken."

Cortez came promptly with Doña Marina and five captains. Juan took his place beside Montezuma.

"The gods have spoken," said the emperor. "You must believe me when I say I am sorry at what they order. But we have no choice. We must destroy you or drive you back to the sea. I am warning you so that you may leave the city before this war begins. Go now or you will all be killed."

Cortez thanked him for the warning. "We would be happy to leave, but we have no ships and it will take time to build them."

After much debate Montezuma agreed to use his power to pacify the gods and restrain the priests until ships could be built.

"But I warn you, leave quickly if you wish to live."

Cortez sent two men, one a master shipbuilder, to Vera Cruz. Montezuma's carpenters accompanied them. At the palace all guards were doubled. Horses remained saddled and the men slept fitfully, jumping to arms at every noise. Juan resumed his practice with the crossbow, managing an hour with his father each afternoon when Montezuma rested. Two weeks after the carpenters left he returned from practice in time to overhear the end of a report to Montezuma.

"And they promise to free you when they have killed the Castilians or sent them back to where they came from."

Messengers and emperor were engrossed in a record book unfolded on the floor. Juan backed silently out the door and down the passage. He called Boba loudly and re-entered the room. Montezuma looked up with a smile.

"Come and look. It is good news."

From experience Juan knew the picture records didn't lie. Newly arrived at Vera Cruz were eighteen ships bearing eight hundred men, eighty horses, and five long-robed figures that might be priests. From the message he'd overheard there was no doubt they'd been sent by Governor Velásquez. His father was right. They were caught between the fire and a hot iron.

Chapter Eleven

BESIEGED

It's MADNESS. Two hundred and sixty men to fight Narváez's eight hundred." Ortega prowled the room red-eyed and gaunt from lack of sleep.

"We have fought against greater odds and won," Juan reminded him.

"We weren't fighting against Castilian steel. This cotton armor will be small protection now." His fingers dug into his beard. He sighed. "Yet to sit here and do nothing while Montezuma plots with Narváez would be certain death. It may well be anyway for those who stay."

Juan sat against the wall, his crossbow balanced on his knees, and said nothing. His father had been going round the same circles for days, ever since Cortez had decided to march to Cempoala. The gold ship sent to King Charles had indeed stopped at Cuba. It had eluded Velásquez's attempts to detain it, but the damage had been done. The governor was furious at Cortez's attempts to by-pass him. The army Narváez had led to Cempoala had only one order: destroy Cortez.

The commander had decided to repeat the strategy that had won at Cholula. Attack first. Ortega was ordered to accompany Cortez. Juan was remaining at the palace, no longer Montezuma's page but a bowman. For a share of Ortega's gold one of the less skillful bowmen had willingly returned to the lance and shield. Juan had spent long hours returning the bow to satisfactory working order. It was now a weapon that would serve him well.

"When did we sail from Cuba?" asked Ortega.

"February," said Juan.

"This is the second May. More than a year and we're worse off than before. I should have listened to your Aunt Maria." He halted before Juan and his voice lowered. "If we lose to Narváez, you know what will happen here?"

"I know."

"Don't let them take you alive."

"Never fear, their gods wouldn't accept me as sacrifice." He rose and embraced his father.

"May God and the saints protect you," said Ortega.

"Go with God." A few moments later Juan repeated the farewell to Mateo. Cortez rode out, followed by his ragged army. He left the city of Mexico in the uncertain hands of Pedro de Alvarado. Eighty soldiers, most of them Velásquez men, and four hundred Tlaxcalans remained in the palace.

The weeks that followed stretched everyone's nerves to the brink of madness. More than one soldier prayed for an attack to relieve the agonizing strain of waiting. Then Alvarado yielded to Montezuma's demands and granted the

142

Mexicans permission to hold their annual festival in honor of one of their gods. The tension in the city eased as the Indians prepared a huge idol of dough-covered wood, clothed and decorated with jade and colored strips of paper. From the roof of the palace the soldiers watched the figure being placed in the courtyard of the pyramid across the plaza. Caciques and warriors crowded into the city. A rumor spread that the two sharpened poles erected near the temple were to hold heads of Castilian soldiers.

The snakeskin drum of the temple boomed. Juan and Diego joined others on the highest roof and looked down into the walled plaza around the pyramid. The two-toned drums struck a quick rhythm. Men in feathered headdresses and embroidered costumes formed a circle. Their metal rattles tinkled a counter rhythm to the drums. They circled one way, then the other, into the circle and out. Their feet flashed in perfect unison, each gesture and turn perfectly timed. The patterns became more intricate. Girls with red-feathered arms danced in and out of the circle. Not a single misstep marred the perfect symmetry of the dance. The cadence quickened. Colors blurred. Then the pattern broke, scattering in bits and pieces as a company of Castilians burst into the square.

"They're attacking," cried Diego.

"Not with just one company," said one of the captains. "But it's certainly not a social call. Alvarado has something planned."

They watched the soldiers run back toward the palace,

dragging two Indian youths with them. Alvarado summoned Juan to question the prisoners. After a long night and a promise of freedom, the two captives admitted they had been selected as sacrifices for the gods. The festival would last twenty days and then, they boasted, the Castilians would be destroyed.

Alvarado turned to the listening captains. "I said they were planning to attack. Now do you believe me?"

The captains nodded slowly as they glared at the prisoners.

"We are already well fortified," said one of the captains. "What more can we do?"

Alvarado laughed. "What did we do at Cholula? We are not sheep to wait here for slaughter."

Juan lingered until he was sure the young Indians were passed out of the palace gates as promised. Then he shouldered his crossbow and climbed wearily to his sentry post on the wall. Diego was already there, pacing awkwardly under the weight of broadsword and battered helmet.

"Can you use that thing?" Juan asked.

Diego stiffened. "You saw me practicing in Santiago."

"I hope you've improved since then." He rubbed his burning eyes. "Forgive me, Diego. I've had no sleep."

They walked away from each other along the wall, turned and paced back. When they met again Diego asked, "What is going to happen now?"

"I don't know."

"Didn't Alvarado say anything?"

"He just repeated what Cortez said at Cholula: 'We are not sheep to wait here for slaughter.' "

"Unfortunately Alvarado is no Cortez."

Juan smiled grimly as he walked away. Now that the Velásquez men were about to be rid of the traitorous Cortez, they realized no one else could spring them from this trap with whole skins.

A sharp exclamation took him back to Diego. The last of the Castilian army was disappearing through the gate to the temple court.

"Every soldier except the ones on sentry duty," said the page. "Alvarado's attacking this time."

"If he stops the sacrifice they'll swarm over this building like angry wasps."

"Look." Diego pointed to a figure slowly mounting the pyramid steps. "Isn't that one of the Indians you questioned?"

"Yes."

"But he could have escaped. He was free."

"Not really." Because of his time with Montezuma Juan understood how completely the Mexicans bowed to the will of their gods. "Didn't the Christians walk to meet the Roman lions?"

"That was different. These are the devil's idols."

"But the faith is just as strong."

"That sounds like heresy." The page turned quickly away.

Screams rose from the temple but not from the figure near the top. The priests rushed past the victim and down the steps. From his place on the wall Juan could see nothing of the battle at the foot of the pyramid. Indians ran from the temple court, then the Castilians pounded across the square to the palace.

"Erect the barricades," shouted Alvarado. "We have fallen on those devils as they meant to fall on us."

The warriors who had gathered for the festival collected arms and swarmed into the plaza. Juan swiveled his crossbow from one body to another, seeking a target that wasn't human. Shooting a padded tree trunk was one thing; these were *men*. A spear brushed his helmet and a rock chipped the battlement before him. A screaming Indian raised his spear. Juan fired and the Indian crumpled. Again and again Juan loaded and fired.

They beat the Indians off the walls with lances and swords. The cannon had no effect. The hole left by ball and grapeshot was immediately filled by more warriors. Then the storm of rocks and arrows died. Montezuma stood on the wall, Alvarado and his captains at his side.

Juan slumped to the roof. If he did not rest he wouldn't have strength to wind his crossbow when the attack resumed. But Montezuma persuaded the Indians to withdraw. Juan stretched out and slept where he lay.

The next day the Indians attacked again. After three

hours of steady fighting Alvarado spun Juan away from the wall.

"Get that Mexican dog up here," he shouted.

"Are you speaking of the lord Montezuma?" Juan's voice was icy.

"Fetch him."

Before he could put himself in chains by telling the officer to get Montezuma himself, a rock struck Juan between the shoulder blades. He sprawled breathless on his face. It seemed hours before he could take normal breaths. His muscles would keep him in agony for days, but no bones were broken. He sat up and saw Alvarado leading Montezuma to the wall.

The Indians began shouting, "Set him free. Free Montezuma."

Alvarado drew his dagger and pressed the point against the emperor's chest. "Get them to withdraw or you die."

The fighting stopped, but the Indians didn't withdraw. They settled down around the palace and waited for the Castilians to starve.

Twenty-three days later the Castilians were drinking their daily gourdful of grain boiled with roots and tubers dug from the garden, when the sentry raised a cry.

"Cortez! Cortez is coming!"

They crowded the roofs to watch. At first the increased number of soldiers alarmed them. Was Narváez coming to take command? Then, as the besieging Indians vanished and the large army moved slowly over the causeway, even the dullest eyes could distinguish the commander riding with his captains. Somehow Cortez had defeated Narváez and added the new forces to his own.

Horse hoofs echoed in the deserted streets. Juan hurried to help open the barricade. He waited impatiently for Cortez and the cavalry to enter, then scanned the faces of the foot soldiers.

"Father!"

Ortega embraced him. Juan winced at the pressure on his still tender back. Ortega drew away and frowned at the bandage on his son's head.

"You are wounded."

"Only a few bruises and a huge empty space where my stomach should be. Did you bring food?"

Ortega shook his head. "An army this size is like a plague of locusts. Besides, we weren't any too welcome on our march here."

"But you won."

"Yes, one night's battle and a generous salting of gold and they were ours."

"*Our* gold," grumbled a familiar voice, and Juan's sore back suffered Mateo's embrace.

They had finished swapping accounts of the past month before Diego stepped from the captains' quarters and called. He walked toward them with the gait of one accustomed to the swing of a heavy broadsword. Mateo stared at the weapon.

"Does your uncle know you're playing soldier?"

"Take care," Juan warned. "Diego knows how to use that sword, but you must take my word for it. The Mexicans who felt it no longer speak."

The former page was too full of his news to notice Mateo's welcoming grin. "You should have heard Cortez. He called Alvarado a bungler, said he'd never heard of such stupidity. Doña Marina assured him the festival was not a preparation for war and Alvarado's questioning had merely goaded the boys into making a threat of destruction. Cortez raved and said he wished to God that Montezuma had escaped."

"Thank God Cortez has returned," said Juan. "At least we have a chance now."

The palace now held thirteen hundred soldiers, ninety horses and two thousand Tlaxcalan allies. The Mexicans were determined to destroy them all. The attacks after the disrupted festival were friendly jousts compared to what they launched the day after Cortez returned.

During the siege warriors had gathered from all the provinces. They set fire to the wooden framework of the palace. The Castilians had no choice but to knock out the flaming wall. Indians poured through the opening. Lances, swords and cannon could not stop them. For every fifty Indians that died a hundred took their place. Juan grabbed a sword from a dead soldier and fought through smoke-filled rooms. Boba charged and tore at his attackers and together they survived. At night Juan helped reseal the breaks in the wall only to have it rammed down again the next day.

Cortez sent Juan and Father Olmedo to ask Montezuma to order the fighting stopped so the Castilians could leave the city. Juan was shocked at the change in the emperor. It wasn't the loss of weight so much as the glaze on his eyes, the lack of interest in anything about him. Juan wasn't sure his words were heard until the emperor replied.

"How much more does he want of me? I have done all he asked, but I will not listen to him again. I no longer want to live under the fate he has brought me."

Juan pleaded. Montezuma gazed at him sadly.

"My young friend, I can do nothing even if I wished. They have selected another to fill my place."

"They can't. You are the emperor."

"I was chosen by the council. Now the council has chosen another." His voice regained some of its former sternness. "Even if I had power left, they would not listen. The gods have ordered all of you destroyed."

Juan's chin rose defiantly. "God will not permit it."

A look of hopeless despair flashed over Montezuma's face and was gone almost before Juan could be sure of what he'd seen. The emperor rose.

"I will speak to my people."

When he appeared the hooting and shouting ceased. Four

caciques came forward to where they could speak with the emperor.

"We must tell you that we have chosen Cuernavaca of Ixtapalapa to fill your place. Forgive us, for we have sworn not to stop fighting until every Castilian is slain."

They had scarcely finished speaking when a shower of stones and spears fell over the wall. Montezuma was struck by three stones, one on the head, another on the arm, and the third on the leg. Juan helped carry him to his rooms. For three days he lay quietly, refusing to eat or drink. If he spoke, only the nobles attending him knew. When Father Olmedo brought the inevitable news, Juan leaned against the battlement and wept.

Cortez sent the body to the Mexicans, but the Indians shouted that the Castilians should not worry about Montezuma's burial or anything else. They would soon be dead.

The bridges were gone from the causeways. Twice Cortez led his forces out to replace them, but they could not hold against the Indian forces. As soon as they retreated to the palace the precious bridges were destroyed. Even at night they had no peace. Stones thudded into the open courts until crossing them was like walking through an old quarry. Arrows were as thick as reeds, and the Indians hooted, whistled, drummed, and shouted insults through the night. Juan was soon numb even to their threats of the sacrificial stone.

The soldiers built four movable towers with slits for bowmen and arquebusiers. To Juan's relief his father was not chosen for the attack on the Great Pyramid. Cortez, his shield lashed to his wounded left arm, led the charge after the towers had cleared the way. Juan was certain God intervened, for in no other way could they have fought four thousand Indians up the high, steep steps of the pyramid. The cross and image of Our Lady were gone. Cortez ordered the idols smashed and set fire to the two temples. Then bearing two priests with them as hostages, they fought their way down, tumbling six or ten steps at a time. Though the towers were demolished, they fought their way back to the palace.

Every night graves were added to the garden. There was no one without wounds. Ortega limped; Mateo had lost a slice of ear; Diego had seven cuts to prove he'd truly used his broadsword; Boba's fur was splotched brown with dried blood, not all her own; Juan suffered two broken fingers and a mass of blue-green bruises from the rocks that were harder to dodge than spears. They lay together in the early dawn, listening to the Narváez men curse Cortez, Narváez, and Governor Velásquez. Mateo didn't even look at Diego. Like the rest of them he was too sore, weary, and hungry to waste strength on anything except survival.

The sound of hammering roused them briefly from their stupor.

"More useless war machines," guessed Mateo.

"I wonder." Diego pushed himself to his feet. "I think I will pay a visit to my uncle before our daily visitors arrive."

"You'd better hurry. The drums are already beating." The sounds of impending attack no longer jerked Juan to his feet. Each second of rest was as precious as a mouthful of food. Even Boba refused to stir until the alarm sounded or Juan called.

Diego came rushing back, eyes shining. "We're leaving Mexico tonight."

"How?" asked Mateo. "Is St. Francis growing us wings?"

"No, Cortez is building a bridge."

"We tried that before. Fast as we build them the Indians tear them down."

"Not out there, you dimwitted beetle. Here, in the palace. We carry it with us right across the Tacuba causeway."

Ortega sat up. "Yes, it is a chance."

Not until then did Juan realize that his father had thought there was no chance at all. Even his own small surge of hope was tempered with doubt.

Houses lined one side of the causeway and canoes could attack on the other. Once they were strung out along the causeway even their shields would give no protection. Never before had the familiar "Go with God" held more meaning.

Chapter Twelve

MEXICO LOST

THE PILE of gold bars glowed dully in the torchlight. Jewels sparkled in boxes and across the floor where they'd fallen during the weighing out of the royal fifth. When the king's share had been loaded onto eight horses and the back packs of nearly ninety Tlaxcalans, Cortez turned to the watching soldiers.

"There is over seven hundred thousand pesos worth left. I can do nothing about it. Any soldier who wants it may take it. Otherwise it will be lost to the Mexicans."

Hunger and wounds were forgotten as soldiers scrambled for the gold bars.

"Come," shouted Mateo. He stuffed gold bars into his boots, inside his armor and breeches, and then used his helmet for a jewel bucket. "Hurry, Juan. It will soon be gone."

"Fools," snorted Ortega. "Don't they know they may have to fight or swim? No!" His fingers dug into Juan's arm.

"I'll take no gold." Juan dove into the threshing maze of

arms and legs, snatched a handful of green stones from a box, fought his way back to his father and showed him the jade. "*Chalchihuitles*. The emperor said each was worth twenty loads of gold and they weigh almost nothing."

The order of march was announced. The king's treasure was placed in the center, soldiers and Tlaxcalans divided front and rear. Father Olmedo led them in prayer, and at midnight the forty men carrying the bridge led the way into the mist and drizzle. Ortega was one of the hundred and fifty assigned to guard it. Juan and Diego were together farther back near the treasure. Boba, all ribs and jaws, trotted between them. Mateo was with the rear guard.

They crept through the dark streets, ears and eyes straining. The mist thickened as they neared the causeway. The gold-laden horses were crossing the portable bridge when horns and whistles sounded the alarm. Mexicans swarmed from the lake like mosquitoes, canoes flooding warriors onto the causeway. Juan fired. Before he could reload, a warrior bore down with a lance. Juan dodged and rammed the crossbow into his face.

A canoe unloaded in their path. Juan drew One-Eye's dagger. Diego's sword slashed. Boba leaped for an Indian's arm and Juan stabbed with the dagger. They teamed against another but five more Indians crowded forward. As Juan sent the dog against one, the pack horses charged through. One skidded on the slippery paving and careened into their battle. The horse's terrorized struggles carried all but one

Indian with her into the lake. With Diego's help Juan sent the remaining Mexican over the side of the causeway.

"Follow the horses," Juan yelled.

They raced on. The bridge had been abandoned by the soldiers and the Mexicans had gathered at the rest of the openings to cut down the men as they swam. Diego stopped at the edge of the paving.

"Stay with the horses or we're lost." Juan shoved the page into the water and plunged after him. The water came only to his chest.

"Dear Mother of God," he gasped as he waded toward the next section of causeway. The openings were being bridged with bodies. He had no time to wonder whose. Diego's hesitation had lost them the protection of the horses. Mexicans in canoes speared the floundering Castilians like fish. One took aim at Diego but the page flopped about so wildly the spear missed. Juan seized the end of the weapon and heaved. As the spearman fell backward, the canoe tipped.

"Out into the lake," Juan ordered. "It's our only chance."

"I can't swim!"

"Take a deep breath and hang onto me."

Even with Diego's dragging weight Juan could have swum underwater beyond the tightly packed canoes but he had no breath to spare fighting the page. When Diego began struggling, Juan had to surface or be drowned. He broke water and filled his lungs. Diego clunged to him, gasping with his terror of the water. Then his head fell on Juan's shoulder and an arrow sprouted from his back.

A canoe floated just within bowshot. Juan made a few quiet strokes and the canoe was only a dark shadow in the fog. Supporting the unconscious Diego, Juan trod water and hoped the Indian had not noticed there were two people in the water. It must have been a latecomer to the battle, for after the canoe faded from sight they were alone in the fog. Alone and lost, for Juan no longer had the noise of battle to guide him. Either it was over or he was too far out in the lake to hear.

With Diego to tow he couldn't afford to waste his strength swimming aimlessly. He trod water and prayed. He prayed for guidance. He prayed for his legs not to numb in the icy water, and then he simply said the Ave Maria over and over, not even aware he was praying aloud until Boba barked.

"Here, girl." The angular head sailed smoothly out of the fog. Juan sobbed with relief. "Don't jump on me, you dunce. You want to drown me?"

Not until she'd expressed her joy by ducking him and then licking his sputtering face did the greyhound strike off into the fog at a slight angle to the direction from which she'd come. Juan hesitated, wondering if she was guiding him back to the bridge. But he had no choice. It was trust the dog or drown. He broke off the protruding arrow shaft, slipped his arm around Diego, and followed.

Without the sight of land to mark their progress the distance seemed endless. Juan's rest periods grew longer and came closer together. Dragging an unconscious Diego was strain enough, but as he slowly regained his senses, the page resumed his frantic struggling and became a real danger. Juan threatened to abandon him if he didn't relax and stop fighting. After that, Diego was quiet but his body remained tense with fear.

Boba swam twice as far as Juan, for she would disappear into the mist when he trod water, then return and swim around him until he was ready to continue. Juan's muscles numbed. He willed them to move. Suddenly Diego pushed away.

"No!" Juan reached for him, struggling to keep afloat, then felt the mud beneath his feet. Diego staggered against him and they waded ashore supporting each other.

"Don't stop," Juan ordered. "Keep moving."

The mist turned to drizzling rain as they plodded toward higher ground. Boba stopped. Her ears stiffened, her nose twitched. With a yelp she raced off. They staggered after her, unable to part without falling. They saw the fires and the familiar figures around them.

"But where are the rest?" said Diego.

Less than a third of the men who'd left the palace moved around the fires. They rested against each other, Diego weak from loss of blood and Juan exhausted from the waters. Near them a man hunched against a cypress tree.

"My father," said Juan. "He mourns for me."

But as they moved closer he saw it was not Ortega. The man's shoulders trembled and more than drizzly rain wet his face. Gently Juan steered Diego away from the cloaked figure.

"It is Cortez," he whispered. "He weeps for us all."

Over eight hundred Castilians and twelve hundred Tlaxcalans were lost at the bridges. In the watery spaces of the causeway lay also the horses and Indians who had carried the treasure, and somewhere among the dead rested Mateo with his boots of gold.

Juan's father lived but his leg wound was a swollen angry red. He insisted on walking. Juan cut him a staff but Ortega soon joined Diego across the rump of a wounded horse. The page had mercifully fainted during the removal of the arrow and the searing of the flesh, but he swore it was the treatment, not the wound, that caused his pain and weakness. Juan was ashamed to march unmarked but he needn't have worried. He soon had painful wounds of his own, though none as serious as Diego's.

The retreat to Tlaxcala was a nightmare. All cannon, powder and most of the crossbows had been lost on the causeway. Their stomachs were two days empty when they started and if harassing Indians had not killed one of the priceless horses they'd have had nothing to eat for a third. They'd fled from Mexico on the night of June thirtieth. On July eighth they fought their way over the mountains and reached the first of the friendly Tlaxcalan towns. There they rested, ate, and cared for their wounds.

Diego was again on his feet, but Ortega's leg was past saving. There was no time to rest after the amputation. Juan's father was placed on a hastily contrived litter, feverish and unconscious. For a while Father Olmedo feared for his life, but as they neared Tlaxcala Ortega was leaning eagerly over the side of the litter to inspect the fields. As they filed through the streets to their quarters Juan heard a harsh voice berating the clumsiness of those helping the wounded. He stared down at his father.

"It can't be."

Ortega flushed guiltily. "I meant to tell you when I returned from Vera Cruz but it slipped my mind."

Juan remembered the five long-robed figures in the picture records. They weren't priests but women, and Aunt Maria was one of them. Juan's inexperience with a sword had left him as battle-scarred as Díaz, but those badges of valor made no impression on Aunt Maria. She treated both Juan and his father as helpless infants.

It was more than a year before Juan saw Mexico again. It had been a year of mutiny, battle and revolution. Cortez had fought with steel in this new land and with words in the court of Castile. And the lawyer had won. He had fought his way back to Mexico and laid siege to the city on the lake. During the months it took to starve Mexico into surrender

Juan helped his father establish their plantation at Tlaxcala. Aunt Maria received word that her new husband, a Narváez captain, had been made governor of a city on the lake shore. Juan escorted her to her new home. When they arrived the conquest was over. The great city whose splendor had awed the Castilians lay in rubble.

Mexico was dead and not even the great pyramids were to be left to mark the grave. Already the stones were being pulled down to build a church.

"It seems fitting," Father Olmedo told him.

"A symbol of God's triumph over the devil," said Diego. A year's campaigning under Cortez hadn't completely erased his air of smugness.

"But so much here was beautiful," said Juan. "Once it's destroyed it can never be again."

"That is the way of growth," said Father Olmedo. "What happens to youth? Is it not destroyed by the process of growing? You have only one childhood. Once its numbered years have passed it can never exist again. No matter how happy it might have been, would you renounce manhood to keep the ways of a child?"

Diego laughed. "Of course not."

"I don't know." Juan frowned. "I think often of the days in Cuba and it doesn't seem to be *me* I remember but some boy I once knew. I haven't grown the way Boba grew larger from a puppy to a dog. I've become a different person, a stranger."

"Look." The priest pointed to the busy masons. "Those stones are forming a church, but they are the same stones that formed the pyramid. Their size and shape dictate the way the church must be built and the hands that set them are not Castilian but Mexican."

Diego snorted. "If we are to have an Indian church we might just as well have let the temple stand."

"No, Diego, we could not let it stand. Everything must grow and change." Father Olmedo looked thoughtfully at Juan. "The new city will not be another Castile. Montezuma's people will mold and shape it into something new and different. However strange it may look to you, Juan, the old Mexico will always be part of it just as that child in Cuba will always be part of you."

Perhaps the priest was right. Hadn't the dreams and loneliness of that boy in Cuba driven him to this new land? If he had remained in Santiago—but that boy couldn't have stayed. His very nature had forced him to seek his first true companion.

Now Boba was in Tlaxcala, too stiff from old wounds to follow her master any distance, and Juan himself ached from invisible wounds. These past years had chipped away the boy bit by bit just as the masons shaped the stones to fit. It hurt and it was frightening. What kind of Juan was being shaped to fit into the world of men?

He watched a massive stone being fitted against its neighbor. One side was dark with dried blood. It would be hidden by the next stone, but it would always be there just as the boy from Cuba and his dreams and fears would always be somewhere in the new older Juan.

Father Olmedo was right. The Castilians would build their new city, but the Mexico from which it sprang would mold and shape its growth. Wherever he went Juan would take that knowledge with him for comfort, but he would not come again to the city on the lake.

He turned sadly away. He knew for himself how painful was the growth from child to man. He could not bear to watch.

Bibliography

Díaz del Castillo, Bernal, *The Bernal Díaz Chronicles,* Albert Idell, ed. Garden City, New York, Doubleday & Co., 1956.

Horgan, Paul, *Conquistadors in North American History.* New York, Farrar, Straus & Co., 1956.

Madariaga, Salvador de, *Hernán Cortés, Conqueror of Mexico.* New York, The Macmillan Co., 1941.

Soustelle, Jacques, *Daily Life Among the Aztecs.* New York, The Macmillan Co., 1962.

Vaillant, G. C., *The Aztecs of Mexico.* Baltimore, Maryland, Penguin Books, 1950.

Von Hagen, Victor W., *The Aztec: Man and Tribe.* New York, Mentor Books, 1958.

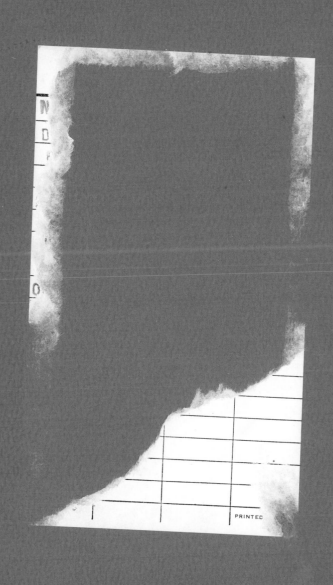